PUFFIN BOOKS
THE COURAGE OF ANDY ROBSON

All his life Andy Robson had lived with the lights and the sounds of the Sleetburn colliery, the noise of the cage clanging to the surface, the buzzers, and the steps of men going to and from work in their heavy boots. Now, transplanted far north to stay with his aunt and uncle following his father's terrible accident in the mine, Andy felt lost and lonely in the quietness of the country. It wasn't just the sounds that were different, either. Andy found that there were many things in his new life that he would have to get used to, both at home and at school.

Andy's Uncle Adam was Park Warden to Lord Hetherington's estate and so responsible for the wellbeing of the famous wild white cattle of Lilburn. His work wasn't made any easier by the rude and uncaring attitude of Lord Hetherington himself, who regarded the cattle as an expensive nuisance and Uncle Adam's requests as mere irritations. Then disaster struck – not just once, but twice – and Andy found himself forced to draw on reserves of strength and courage that he hadn't realized he possessed.

Frederick Grice's story of bravery in many forms, which has recently been adapted for television, will be enjoyed by readers of ten and over. Another novel by Frederick Grice with a similar mining background is also published in Puffins: *The Bonny Pit Laddie*.

~FREDERICK GRICE~

The
Courage of Andy Robson

PUFFIN BOOKS
in association with Oxford University Press

Puffin Books, Penguin Books Ltd, Harmondsworth, Middlesex, England
Penguin Books, 625 Madison Avenue, New York, New York 10022, USA
Penguin Books Australia Ltd, Ringwood, Victoria, Australia
Penguin Books Canada Ltd, 2801 John Street, Markham, Ontario, Canada L3R 1B4
Penguin Books (N.Z.) Ltd, 182–190 Wairau Road, Auckland 10, New Zealand

First published by Oxford University Press 1969
Published in Puffin Books 1982

Printed and bound in Great Britain by
Cox & Wyman Ltd, Reading
Set in Linotron 202 Plantin by
Rowland Phototypesetting Ltd
Bury St Edmunds, Suffolk

To the memory of
my dear mother

⁓Contents⁓

Leaving Home

'Thanks very much for bringing me to the station, Mr Barnes,' said Andrew. He was looking out through the open window of the railway carriage and down on to Mr Barnes's cap. The early morning mist through which they had driven had left the rough tweed covered with hundreds of tiny globes of moisture.

'It was no trouble, hinny,' said Mr Barnes, pulling out his watch and checking it with the station clock, 'I had to come to Durham in any case. Dinna forget that you have to change at Newcastle Central for Alnwick. Did you remember to bring something to eat on the train?'

'Yes, Mr Barnes.'

'Put your bass up on the rack then and it winna get in the way of anybody.'

Mr Barnes, like Andrew's father and mother, lived at Sleetburn, but he did not work in the pit. He had a ramshackle stable at the bottom of the colliery, with two horses and a trap. In the yard outside the stable he had also a flat cart that he called a 'rolly', and a second cart with sides. He made his living by moving furniture, delivering coals for the colliery management, and taking people to Durham on Saturdays. He had come to Sleetburn from Northumberland, and that was how he came to be friends with Andrew's father and mother, because Mrs Robson had come from Berwick to be a maid at Brancepeth Castle, and it was when she was there that she met her husband who was working in the pit at Sleetburn.

Although Andrew was a miner's son and would probably have to work in the pit himself when he was old enough, he listened with only half an ear when he heard his father talking with his mates about pit-work. He liked best to be with Mr Barnes, yoking and unyoking the horses, rubbing them down, cleaning out the stables, forking hay into the mangers, and going with him when he had to collect or deliver a load. He was happy in Sleetburn, but Mr Barnes and his two horses meant more to him than all the rest of the colliery.

While they were waiting for the train to go out they heard the horse whinnying in the station yard. 'Listen to that gallowa,' said Mr Barnes, 'he's worse than a bairn. If he's left by hisself for a few minutes he thinks I've left him for good.'

'Do you think it will be a long time before I can come home?' asked Andrew.

'Dear knows. Your father's had a bad knock. They'll look after him in the Infirmary, and it winna be long afore he's on his feet again. But it's bound to be a few months before he can manage properly. There's the whistle. Shut that window when the train starts. If you keep poking your head out like that you'll finish up in the Infirmary as well. Look after yourself now, and don't worry about your mother. We'll take care of her.'

The engine gave a jerk, paused, and gave a second jerk. The buffers went cannoning against one another, as if some message was being passed along the train. Andrew could hear the horse whinnying in the yard as if it was begging him not to go but to jump out and stay; but the platform slid away, dipped, and was gone. He watched Mr Barnes go through the barrier and out of sight. Then he lifted his bass on to the rack and sat down.

The compartment was not empty. Opposite him in the far corner was an old man in a light-coloured suit and a very high white collar. The collar was so high that the folds of his neck sagged over it. He was sitting reading a heavy book. Although it was not hot in the compartment and the morning was still grey with mist, he had taken his hat off, and every now and then passed his hand over his smooth bald head as if he was wiping some dampness from it. Andrew did not dare to look too closely or too long at him. He turned away and looked out of the window, watching the telegraph poles flashing past, and the wire rising and dipping. On the wall opposite him there were three brown photographs with 'Valentine' scrawled in the corners. The titles read 'Blackhall Rocks', 'High Force' and 'The High Level Bridge, Newcastle'. He recognized the bridge but the other places meant nothing to him. When he turned to look out of the window again he saw nothing but colliery slag-heaps and pit-head gear and rows of houses like the houses at Sleetburn where he lived, their blue slate roofs damp in the morning mist. All the while the old man went on reading, turning over the pages very slowly, pressing them down with his mottled hands, and wiping his bald head.

Then the train slowed down and the countryside began to change. The land fell away, and Andrew saw, at an immense distance below him, the wide waters of the Tyne with its quays lined with ships. The train was going over the famous High Level Bridge that Mr Valentine had taken a photograph of, and would soon be at the Central Station. Andrew took down his bass and got ready to get out.

He had a long time to wait for his connection, but once he had found the platform from which his train was to leave he stayed there, asking every porter who came past if this was the platform for the Alnwick train, just to make certain that he was in the right place. He sat down on his bass, looking up from time to time at the vault of the station roof and the pigeons flying from girder to girder. This was the longest train journey he had ever done, and the first he had done on his own. He was beginning to be hungry, but he did not dare begin on the food his mother had given him in case the train came in before he had time to finish it.

When at last it did draw up, he found a compartment to himself. He didn't know whether to stay there or to move. He would have liked someone to be there to assure him that he was on the right train and to tell him when he was getting near Lilburn, but he was hungry and did not want to open his food in the presence of strangers. But just before the train pulled out the door was flung open and a case was pitched in. Andrew recognized the case: it belonged to the old man who had travelled with him from Durham. The old man was in such a fluster that at first he did not see Andrew, but when he had pulled off his hat and wiped his head and leant forward to look over the rims of his metal spectacles, he recognized him.

'Bless me!' he said. 'Aren't you the boy who got in at Durham and travelled here with me?'

'Yes, sir.'

'Well, it looks as if we are fated to be travelling companions, whether we want to or not. What's your name?'

'Andrew Robson.'

'And what are you doing by yourself on this long journey?'

'I'm going to stay with my uncle.'

'For a holiday?'

'No, sir, I'm going to stay with my uncle and aunt till my father comes out of the Infirmary.'

'The hospital, I suppose you mean.'

'No, sir, Durham Infirmary.'

'What's the matter with your father? Is he ill?'

'He had an accident in the pit.'

'What happened to him?'

'The rammel came down and crushed his legs.'

'The rammel? What an extraordinary word! What on earth is the rammel?'

'I think it's the roof, the roof of the seam where the men work.'

'Tell me more about it, Andrew.'

'The rammel?'

'No, the accident.'

'I don't know much more about it. They took my father straight to the Infirmary, and they wouldn't let anybody go and see him except my mother and Mr Barnes.'

'So you're a miner's boy, are you? I suppose you live in one of those dreadful places I saw on my way up on the train.'

'Yes, sir, Sleetburn.'

'Sleetburn? A harsh name – for a harsh place, no doubt. I'm very sorry to hear about your father, but it strikes me as a bit strange that you should be leaving your mother just when she is most likely to need you.'

'There's too many of us to look after. My uncle said I could go and live with him and my Aunt Florrie till my father gets better.'

'And how do you feel about all this? I mean, about leaving Sleetburn and your mother – and your family? Do you want to leave them?'

'No, sir.'

'I can see that you don't. Never mind, Andrew, the chances are that you will be going to a far more pleasant place than Sleetburn. I take it that your father was badly hurt.'

'Mr Barnes says that the rammel crushed both his legs.'

'Who is this Mr Barnes you keep mentioning?'

'He's the man who brought me to Durham in his trap.'

'I'm sorry to hear about the accident, Andrew. You almost make me ashamed of myself with nothing to do but follow my own pleasant little hobbies while men like your father are risking their limbs to keep us warm. The least I can do is to make your journey a pleasant one. Have you something to eat?'

'Yes, sir.'

'So have I, and something tells me it's time for refreshment. Let's settle down and enjoy our lunch, shall we? Have you anything to drink?'

'No, sir.'

'Never mind. I've something that will do – no, not that,' he said, looking at a silver-topped flask he had taken from his pocket. 'You're a bit young for that. This will do – a bottle of Harrogate water. We'll drink a toast to your father's recovery, and a pleasant stay for you with your uncle, wherever he lives.'

They opened their packages and began to eat. The old man gave Andrew a few chicken sandwiches, and in return took a piece of Mrs Robson's bacon and egg pie. Andrew did not care very much for the Harrogate water; neither, for that matter, did the old man, who found whatever there was in the flask much more enjoyable.

When they had finished, the stranger brushed the crumbs from his waistcoat and wiped his moustache with his hanky.

'It has just struck me, Andrew,' he said, 'that I haven't yet asked you where you are going. Where exactly does your uncle live?'

'In Lilburn.'

'But that's where I'm going!'

'Are you going there for a holiday?'

'In a sense yes, and in a sense no. My life is all one long holiday or one long grind – it all depends how you look at it. I'm an artist, a painter of landscapes and great houses, and things like that. The Lord of Lilburn – Lord Hetherington I suppose I ought to call him – has asked me to do a view of his castle. But that's not what I'm really after.'

'No?'

'No. Lord Hetherington does not know, but I'm more interested in his cattle than his castle . . . I dare say that just sounds like a feeble joke to you, Andrew. But you may see the sense of it later. In the meanwhile I'm going to have a little nap. It's a good thing we are going to the same place. I can take a nap and still make sure of getting off at the right station. You won't forget to waken me, will you? Here, you take my book. It was written by a man who was a greater artist than ever I'll be, I fear. You take a look at that, and I'll drop off for a few minutes.'

He leant his head against the corner padding of the compartment and fell asleep. Andrew took up his book and began to look idly through it. It wasn't a story book. It was called *The History of Quadrupeds*, and contained a large number of illustrations. There was even one of a bull from the herd of Lilburn White Cattle, but neither this nor any of the other illustrations meant much to Andrew. He put down the book and looked out of the window.

The morning mist had dispersed and everything shone in the summer sunlight. On one side the landscape was green and undulating, with no slag-heaps now to break the skyline, no pit-head gear or rows of brick houses, but stone farmsteads surrounded by meadows and plough-land. On the other side, however, the land was rising into dark, rounded hills higher than any Andrew had ever seen, their shadowed summits streaked with snow that still lay unmelted in the high gullies. As the train drove through the quiet, lonely countryside the horses and cattle in the fields shied away from the noise as if they had never seen engine or carriages before.

Station followed station, the old man sleeping steadily through the afternoon, until Andrew heard a voice calling in a rough, unfamiliar accent, 'Lilborn! Lilborn!' He woke the old man and they both scrambled out.

They were the only two passengers to alight, and there was

only one man waiting for them. Andrew knew it was his uncle. He had never seen him before but he knew that this man with the dark-brown eyes and the long thin nose was his mother's brother.

'Weel, Andrew,' said his uncle. His voice sounded Scottish and he pronounced the name more like 'Andrer' than Andrew. 'Ye've arrived safe and sound. Nae need for to have a label roond your neck. I'd pick ye oot of a hundred. Is this your baggage?'

'Yes, Uncle.'

'You're in luck's way today, bonny lad. Hetherington sent me doon to pick up anither gentleman from the train. Ye'll be the man I'm looking for, sir,' he went on, turning to the old man. 'Are ye for Lilburn Castle?'

'That's right, I'm Mr Dennison.'

'Pleased to meet ye, sir. I'm Charlton. You'll no mind if my nephew comes in the trap with us?'

'We've shared a compartment ever since Durham, so I think it will be very fitting for us to finish the trip together. I know all about Andrew's story.'

'Aye, his father and mother have had a bit of gay bad luck, but he'll be weel looked after here. I've got the trap outside, sir.'

'I've been wondering, Charlton,' said Mr Dennison as they went through the barrier, 'if you'll be able to do me another favour. What do they call the man who looks after the famous wild cattle here?'

'The Park Warden, sir.'

'That's the title, is it? Well now, I've come to do a job for Lord Hetherington, but I'm really interested in the cattle, and what I was hoping you might be able to do is to put me in touch with this man. Do you think you can help me?'

'Ye couldna ha' come to a better shop, Mr Dennison,' said Mr Charlton. 'You see, I'm the Park Warden myself.'

2

New Sights and Sounds

The station was a few miles from the castle, but Mr Dennison asked so many questions that Mr Charlton dropped the reins on the pony's back and let it go at its own pace. From time to time snatches of their conversation came to Andrew, talk of heifers and enclosures, pastures and cow-licks, but he was too intent on looking round him to take much in. Everything was new and strange to him: the glossy black cattle; the hedges sprinkled with blackthorn blossom; the black patches of burnt heather on the fellside slopes; and the looming hills with the snow still lying in patches in the shadowy gullies. There were few houses to be seen, but eventually they drove through an avenue of towering trees and stopped beside a pair of massive gates. His uncle told him to get down and wait there till he had taken Mr Dennison to the hall.

When the noise of the trap wheels had died away a quietness that troubled Andrew seemed to fall over everything. The streets of Sleetburn were always full of noise and bustle, but Lilburn seemed empty and deserted, with no women gossiping at the gates, no hawkers bawling up and down the rows, no boys playing, no dogs prowling and fighting. Behind the screen of the trees he could see the vague outline of the castle, its turrets and battlements rising above the leafy tops of the woodland. The cottages were not huddled together in rows as at Sleetburn, but separate and silent, with noiseless smoke spiralling slowly upwards from the brown chimneys. The air had a strange smell, unlike the familiar smell of coal. The only sounds to be heard were the calling of birds in the high trees, the noise of a saw from some shed or other, and the bleating of a flock of sheep.

The sound of the bleating came nearer, and he turned to see a flock being driven past the gates by a man and a boy with two dogs. It was a mixed flock of ewes and lambs, and the ewes were restive. They kept turning on the dogs, driving them away when they came too close to the lambs. The dogs were darting backwards and forwards, turning their heads back to see what the shepherd wanted them to do, their flanks heaving, and their long red tongues lolling from their mouths. As the flock was driven past Andrew drew back and pressed himself against the wall, half afraid that the dogs might take a snack at him. He must have looked scared because the boy looked scornfully at him and said something that Andrew could not catch. He was a fat boy with a red and sweaty face, and as he came past the bass he kicked it out of the way. Andrew flushed, but he was too afraid of the dogs to retaliate. He let the flock go and waited for his uncle to return.

'Ye'll be tired of waiting, I expect,' he said when at last he appeared. 'But I had to see the pony stabled. And if I hadn' rubbed him down Hetherington would ha' been after me. Still, we're nearly hame noo.'

He swung the bass onto his shoulders, and in a few minutes Andrew was safe in his aunt's house, answering all her questions about his father, his mother, himself, and all the family.

The light had not yet drained out of the sky when Mr Charlton lay back in his chair, yawned, and said, 'Weel, Andy, we've had a gay good crack, but enough's as good as a feast. The rest will have to wait till tomorrow. Time for bed now.'

To Andrew's surprise he pulled off his boots, then stripped off his stockings and threw them in the oven. He had never seen anybody put his stockings in the oven before, but his aunt did not think there was anything unusual about her husband's behaviour. She went out for a bucket of peats, built up the fire, and took off her apron.

'We're always off to bed in good time here, Andy,' she said. 'And I daresay you'll be ready for a good sleep after a lang day in the train. We dinna use a candle at this time of the year. You have young eyes and you winna need one.'

Andrew was a little taken aback. His mother and father never went to bed early, and he was used to running the streets for an hour or two before bedtime. Going to bed when it was still light was something he had never done before. He wondered how anyone could go to sleep before it was dark.

He went over to his bedroom window, but a sudden screech from outside made him jump. It sounded to him as if something or someone had suddenly spied him in the unfamiliar room and meant to frighten him away from it. When the sound came again his arms began to pimple with fear. He turned and ran downstairs.

'What was that, Aunt Florrie? That noise?'

'What noise?' asked his aunt. She was kneeling on the hearth brushing the ashes into the fire.

'That noise outside the window. That screeching.'

'Oh,' she said calmly. 'It'll be just an owl, like as not.'

'It didn't sound like an owl. It was a screech.'

'It will be just a screech-owl, hinny. You'll get used to them. The place is wick wi' them.'

'It made me jump, Auntie.'

'Lord above, man, if you're ganna be flayed wi' things like that, ye'll nivver get to sleep. Dinna worry, hinny, they're mair frightened of you than you are of them.'

Andrew went back to his room, but he did not get into bed.

He looked out of the window trying to see the owl, but he could make out nothing but the high, looming shapes of the trees, and the first stars flickering above the topmost branches. In the distance he could hear a dog barking, and the sound of the birds settling for the night. The quietness made him uneasy. He wished he could see the lights and hear the sounds of the colliery, the noise of the cage clanging to the surface, the tankies shunting trucks, the buzzers, and the sluther of men going to and from work in their heavy boots. He felt lost and lonely, and lay for a long time watching the grey rectangle of the window growing darker and darker.

But just before he went to sleep his thoughts changed, and he recalled something his uncle had said to Mr Dennison before they got into the trap.

'I'm the Park Warden myself,' he had said. Andy had hardly noticed the remark at the time, but now it came back to him, and he was still wondering why Mr Dennison had looked so impressed when he fell asleep.

∽3∽

A New Style of Fighting

'Did ye have a good sleep then, hinny?' asked his aunt when Andrew came down the next morning. 'I can see ye did. I popped in when your uncle went out and ye were dead to the world. I've got a nice trout for your breakfast. Ye look to me as if ye could do wi' something filling.'

'Is that your dog, Aunt Florrie?' asked Andrew, looking at a collie stretched out before the fire.

'Yes, that's our Cappy.'

At the sound of its name the dog turned its head and looked up, then lay down with a sigh again.

'He's very quiet.'

'Aye, but he can be gay noisy when he likes, can't you, Cappy?'

The dog wagged its tail as if to indicate that it knew it was being discussed, but made no move to get up. Andrew sat down and began on his breakfast. He had never had fish before at this time of the day. At home he always had bacon.

'What's the matter?' said his aunt, watching him picking at the trout. 'Are ye a bit faddy?'

'It's the bones.'

'Ye'll soon get used to managing them. Have ye finished?'

'Yes, thank you.'

'What are you going to do wi' yourself today?'

'I'll see if I can find anybody to play with.'

'That's a good idea. I canna abide anybody under my feet when I'm cleaning up.'

'Where's Uncle Adam?'

'He's gone off to look at the herd. Find yourself somebody to play wi' till dinner-time.'

'Can I take the dog out?'

'Ye'd better not. Your uncle doesn't like him running wild. He's very biddable, but he's a bit of a mis-stitched yin. Ye'd better not take him till he gets used to you. Dinna be late for dinner, mind, 'cos your uncle doesn't like to be kept waiting.'

The village was still quiet, but there were two boys out playing beside the church wall. They were playing tip-cat, knocking the 'cat' up and down the bare patch of earth between the church and the castle gates. As Andrew got close to them one of the boys knocked the cat in the air, clouted it, and drove it towards him. 'It's a cross,' said Andrew, looking down at the cat. He was pleased to find them playing a game that he knew. 'You're out.'

'What's it got to do wi' ye?' said the bigger of the boys, snatching up the cat.

It was the boy who had kicked Andrew's bass as he had gone past him the night before. He was a big boy, fat rather than tall, with thick shoulders and thick arms. His face was so swollen and fleshy that his eyes looked like raisins in a pasty bun.

'I was just calling out for you,' said Andrew.

'Mind your own business,' said the boy. 'Naebody asked you to put your spoke in.'

He came closer to Andrew and shouldered him away.

Andrew pushed him back, but he quickly dropped both cat and stick, closed on him and grabbed him round the waist. He swept Andrew's legs from under him and sent him sprawling in the dust. Andrew was not used to this kind of attack. He had been in many a fight in his time and knew how to stick up for himself, but the boys of Sleetburn always fought with their fists. He picked himself up and lunged forward, but before he could land a punch, the boy grabbed him again round the waist and sent him sprawling a second time.

'That'll learn ye,' he shouted. 'Clear off back where ye belang! Ye dinna belang here and we dinna want ye!'

Andrew picked himself up again. He was furious at being knocked down so easily. He was no coward. He would take on anybody his own size. But this was a style of fighting that he was not used to and he didn't know how to deal with it. He went back home, and, hearing his aunt busy in the kitchen, sat in the shed where his uncle kept his gardening tools. He was vexed at not being allowed to join in the game, and mortified at having been knocked down so easily. He dusted his clothes and scraped off some of the mud with his finger-nail, but there was a tear in his trousers that he could not hide. He spent the rest of the morning in the shed and in the churchyard until it was time for dinner.

'What have ye been up to then, Andy?' said his uncle. 'Did ye find any lads to play wi'?'

'They wouldn't let me play.'

'Ye look to me as if ye've been in a battle. Turn round. Aye, you've got a tear in your britches. What's up? Have ye been fighting already?'

'He didn't fight properly.'

'Who didn't?'

'I don't know what they call him. A fat boy with piggy eyes.'

'That'll be young Billy Craggs, the gardener's lad. Ye'll have to watch him, Andy. He's always fighting, that lad. He's notorious.'

'He kicked my legs out under me.'

'That's the style in these parts.'

'What style?'

'Wrestling. They dinna fight here, they wrestle. All the lads are daft on wrestling in this place. Ye'll have to learn to wrestle, bonny lad, or else ye'll have nae peace.'

'We fight with our fists in Sleetburn.'

'Maybe, but when ye're in Lilburn ye'll have to wrestle. I should ha' warned ye about that. Just keep out of the way of Billy Craggs till ye've got the knack. He's a good hand at the wrestling and he'll take a lot of beating.'

It was a long day for Andrew. After dinner Mr Charlton went off to see someone at the castle, and his wife went with him to pay her weekly visit to the housekeeper there. Andrew was left alone in the house with a long, empty day before him. He wished he was back at home, going to watch a football match or walking to Durham with his father or helping Mr Barnes with the horses. He walked idly round the house, looking out of the windows like a prisoner.

After a while he went out into the yard and began shying pebbles at a tin that he set up on the pump trough, but as soon as he began Cappy came padding out of the kitchen and stood in the doorway looking quizzically at him. Then suddenly it ran for one of the stones he had thrown and brought it back to him, tossing it down with a playful action.

'Fetch it, boy,' said Andrew, throwing the stone again at the tin. The dog needed no second invitation. It retrieved the stone and tossed it down before him again, lying down with its nose between its paws as if daring him to take the pebble. Andrew took it and threw it this time in the air, but Cappy leapt like a fish and caught it before it hit the ground.

'You're a clever dog, aren't you?' said Andrew. 'You're fed up with being left alone as well, eh?' And as if to signify that it knew exactly what he meant Cappy abandoned the stone and came to him with a short stick, tossing it down before him in an invitation to start a new game.

They played until they were both hot and tired. Then

when Andrew went back into the kitchen Cappy followed him and sat leaning its hot body against his legs, slanting its head and looking at him out of the corners of its eyes.

'My goodness, you two are good friends, I must say,' said Mrs Charlton when she came in and saw them sitting together. 'Have you been playing with him?'

'Yes, we've been playing in the yard.'

'I think he's taken to you, Andrew. He'll be good company for you. He's one of Dickie Ingram's, but he wasn't much use as a sheep-dog.'

'Is that why you called him mis-stitched?'

'That's it. He was nae good wi' the flock, but he's got a good headpiece, haven't you, Cappy? Come on, boy.'

But Cappy did not move. It pressed its body up against Andrew's leg and kept looking up at him.

His new friendship with the dog helped Andrew to forget the humiliation of the morning and gave him new confidence and hope. At supper his uncle told him that Dickie Ingram, Lord Hetherington's shepherd and the man who had given him the dog, was one of the best wrestlers in the county.

'If you want a bit of tuition,' he said, 'he's the man to give it to you. He kens mair about the sport than any man in Northumberland.'

It was too much to expect a champion to give lessons to a colliery boy, but Andrew thought that since he had been kind to Cappy, Mr Ingram might let him watch him. He made up his mind to try to get to know the shepherd and find out what sort of a man he was.

He went to bed early again – and lay awake waiting for the owls. But this time his ears caught a different sound. He did not know what to make of it. It was like the lowing of cattle, but higher-pitched and more defiant. Then he heard the bellowing being answered, another high-pitched, angry note. He thought of going down to ask his aunt what the noise was,

23

but he was afraid of bothering her a second time. He heard his uncle open the kitchen door, go out into the yard, stand there listening, and then come in and lock the door.

Then the sounds died away. Andrew lay waiting for them to begin again and wondering where they came from. He was not used to noises like these and they puzzled him. But neither his uncle nor his aunt seemed to be worried about them, so he pulled the blankets up around his shoulders and went to sleep.

4

Sunday at Lilburn

'I hope Hetherington doesna keep us ower lang this morning, Florrie,' said Mr Charlton as they went into the church. 'I mortally hate hanging round for him to turn up.'

'Well, ye'll just have to be patient, Adam. There's nothing we can do to make him come any quicker.'

Andrew did not know what they were talking about. He was too busy watching what they did because he was not used to going to church. He had been to chapel many a time with Mr Barnes, who was a Methodist, but he had never been inside a proper church. He took the prayer book that his aunt handed to him, knelt down when she knelt and got up when she did. Squinting sideways he saw that she had her book open at the Order for Morning Prayer. It took him a long time to find the place in his own book.

The bell had stopped tolling and the clock had already struck the hour, but no one made any attempt to begin the service. The parson had taken his place at his desk, but he sat down with the air of a man who was used to waiting. Then suddenly Andrew saw the congregation scrambling to their feet, and Lord and Lady Hetherington came down the aisle, followed by Mr Dennison. They made their way to the big box-pew at the front and the parson began the service.

It began disastrously for Andrew. The first hymn was 'Jesu, Lover of my soul', one of his favourites, and he was so relieved to come upon something that he could recognize that he lifted his voice and sang out with a will. He knew only one way of singing hymns, the way they sang in the Primitive Methodist Chapel at Sleetburn – at the top of your voice. But before he had got to the end of the first line he knew he had made another blunder. Two or three villagers in the pews in front of him turned round, and even Lord Hetherington looked round disapprovingly to see who it was that was making the row. His aunt nudged him and he let his voice tail away, and from then on he shambled through the service as best he could. The whole affair was a trial to him. He was not used to following a prayer book and could not understand why the minister read some parts and skipped others. He floundered hopelessly, pretending to read the responses and the confession and the creed, watching his aunt out of the corner of his eye. He was glad when the service was over and began to wonder if he would ever get used to this strange place and its strange ways. He went red when his uncle said to him outside, 'For heaven's sake, dinna let rip on them hymns sae much, Andy. Hetherington disna like folks bawling their heads off in church. Lad,' he went on, a fit of laughter coming over him, 'I thought ye were ganna tak the slates off the roof.'

Andrew was not amused. He was vexed at having made an exhibition of himself, and did not want to be reminded of his blunder. Happily, when he got into the churchyard he saw Mr Dennison smiling and waving at him to go over and see him.

'Well, Andrew, it's nice to see you again. Have you settled in your new home yet?'

'Yes, sir.'

'Not homesick?'

'No, sir,' he replied. He thought it was better to tell a lie than try to explain how unhappy he was. His father had often told him that no matter how miserable he was, it was better to keep his misery to himself rather than burden others with it.

'That's the spirit,' said Mr Dennison. 'But I'm sorry to say that I haven't drawn a single line yet. Not that I don't want to, but my host is for ever dragging me out to look at some horse or dog or other. I have a feeling that he knows I'm not really interested in dogs and foxes and thinks me a bit of a poor fish. To tell the truth, I'm dying to get away from him for a few minutes to get your uncle to show me the herd. You never told me he was the Park Warden.'

'I didn't know myself till I got here.'

'He's the man I really want to talk to. But tell me about yourself for a bit.'

This was the last thing Andrew wanted to do; he preferred to keep his unhappiness to himself. Fortunately he was saved from having to tell more lies by Lord Hetherington himself who came shambling over to them. He was a big, untidy man, with a heavy face and a protruding bottom lip. He had been talking to the man whom Andrew had seen driving the flock of sheep through the village on his first evening at Lilburn. He must have been dressing him down because the man looked white and angry. Lord George dismissed him with a careless gesture and came over to Mr Dennison.

'Come on, Dennison. Don't keep me waiting.'

'I'm sorry, Lord George. I was just having a word with the boy I told you about – the miner's son I met in the train.'

'So you're Charlton's nephew, are you?' asked Lord George putting out his lips petulantly.

'Yes, sir.'

'You ever been here before?'

'No, sir.'

'And was that you bawling at the top of your voice in church?'

'Yes, sir.'

'Well, don't do it, do you hear? I won't have you making a

blaring row like that. You're not in chapel now. Has your uncle told you the rules?'

'Which rules, sir?'

'About the castle – the estate.'

'No, sir. I didn't know there were any rules.'

'Well, there are. And you get them into your head. Keep out of my grounds unless you're on business. Or else you'll get a shot up your backside. And no poaching. If I catch you after my fish or my game I'll have you inside. Do you understand?'

'Yes, sir.'

'Come on then, Dennison. I've done enough hanging around here. I'm hungry and I don't like to be kept waiting for my dinner, especially on Sundays.'

Then he turned and stalked away in a pompous, self-important manner. Andrew decided that, lord or no lord, he was a hateful man. He hated him almost as much as he hated Billy Craggs.

Fortunately something else caught Lord George's notice and Mr Dennison had time for a few words with Mr Charlton.

'I'd take it as a favour, Warden, if you could find an hour or two some time to show me the herd. Is today possible?'

'Today's as good as any, Mr Dennison. I'll be awa' up to take a look at them after dinner. If you'd like to come, ye'll be welcome.'

'Fine. I'm looking forward to it. I'll meet you here. But I'll have to hurry off now. Better not keep his lordship waiting. You know what he's like when he's hungry.'

'Uncle Adam,' asked Andrew when they had got back home, 'what's special about these cattle that you're the Warden of? Why is Mr Dennison so keen to see them?'

'Man alive, do ye mean to say that ye've nivver heard of the famous white cattle of Lilburn?'

28

'No.'

'It beats me what you young fellers do in school nowadays! How many years have you been at your lessons now?'

'Seven. Seven and a bit.'

'Seven years? And not one teacher has said a word about the herd? I canna credit it.'

'It's true, Uncle.'

'It's high time ye were learning then. Here, take a look at this book.'

He lifted the lid of an old office desk that stood in the corner of the kitchen and took out the book.

'This is the same as Mr Dennison's book. He has one just like this.'

'How do you know that?'

'He showed it to me on the train.'

'I thought you said you'd never heard about the cattle.'

'I haven't. He let me look at the book but I didn't read it.'

'Well, read it this time. Here, start at this bit. And if ye haven't finished it by dinner-time, ye can stop in this after-noon and finish it.'

Andrew did not find it easy to read. It was written in a long-winded, old-fashioned style, but he did not like the prospect of having to stay in on a fine day when his uncle and Mr Dennison were up in the park. He kept his nose to the book and learnt how, many centuries ago, the great park had been surrounded by a high stone wall, and a small herd of pure white cattle of ancient breed had been enclosed there. For more than seven hundred years the cattle had lived wild in the park. No other cattle had been allowed there. No one had ever tried to domesticate them. This was their home, and there, wild and separate, they had pastured and bred. In every other part of Britain the ancient breed had died out, but the Lilburn herd had gone on living as they had always lived, the purest herd of white cattle in all the islands, a herd without equal anywhere.

'They're famous, aren't they, Uncle?'

'I should think they are. Ye winna find a herd like them anywhere else in the world.'

'Are you famous as well?'

'Me? There's nowt special about me, hinny. I'm just the feller that looks after them. But sit up and reach to, Andy. Now that you've read about the cattle, ye'd better come and see them. And ye'd better mak a note of it, lad, because you'll be looking at something today that not ivverybody has the good luck to see.'

∽5∽

The Wild Cattle

They found Mr Dennison waiting for them in the church-yard.

'I'm fetching my sister's lad alang wi' me if ye've nae objection. I want him to see the herd as weel.'

'Andrew and I are old friends. It won't be the first thing we've done together, will it?'

'Put your best foot forward then, the pair of ye. It's a stiff climb. Dinna mind if I leave ye behind now and then. I'm used to walking fast and I cannot abide dawdling.'

They went through a gate and began to climb a steep cart track. Mr Charlton went on ahead, striding up the slope in his big, curved shepherd's boots, then paused on the top of the ridge to let them catch up with him. 'There's the park,' he said. 'Take a rest if you're puffed, and I'll see if I can find where the herd has got itself to this afternoon.'

From the rise the ground fell away gently and, about half-way down the slope and a quarter of a mile ahead of them, they saw the big stone wall that Andrew had read about. The low-lying ground beyond the wall was green and fertile, but the far slopes were covered here and there with heather and gorse. Beyond the ridge nothing could be seen but the white and looming clouds.

'I suppose the cattle live out all the year, Mr Charlton,' said Mr Dennison.

'Ye wouldn' get them into a byre. But there's a shelter yonder. Can ye see it? That place yonder.'

He pointed with his stick to a low windowless building on the edge of the pasture.

'Not that they use it much. Ye'll mebbe see them there in very bad weather. But they'd sooner be out in the open. Have you spotted them yet, Andy?'

'There's something there on the edge of the plantation,' said Andrew.

'Aye, that's the deer – and bad cess to them. There's far ower many of them in the park in my opinion. I wish that Hetherington would keep them out. But he's a sackless feller if ever there was one. He thinks mair of them than he does of his cattle. Can ye see anything white?'

'Not yet.'

'Aye, they're a kittle lot. Ye never know where they'll be from one day to the next. We'll have to move on a bit. Are ye ready for another spell, Mr Dennison?'

'I'm ready.'

'Keep on the safe side of the wall, then. We might have to walk right round it afore we see the herd.'

'How far is it?'

'Seven miles from start to finish.'

'Seven miles! . . . That's a lot of wall for a few cattle.'

'There's thirty head of them.'

'That's still not a big herd.'

'It's big enough. And it would ha' been bigger if Hetherington would keep his hands off them. He killed one of them just afore Christmas last year, and another when some sackless friend of his took a fancy to hunting them. I tellt him that he'd kill the lot off one of these days if he didn' show mair sense. But he dissent care. He's got something here that many a man would give a mint of money for. But just try to tell him!'

32

'It seems to me they're difficult enough to find, never mind to hunt.'

'Aye, they're very sweir. We might have to walk to the top of the fell afore we see them.'

'Why can't you climb over the wall and cut across?' asked Andrew.

'What? Do you want to commit suicide? There's one thing you'll have to get into your nut, my lad. Nivver cross this wall. If the cattle spot you, you'll nivver get out alive.'

'Surely they're not as savage as that,' said Mr Dennison.

'These are wild cattle, Mr Dennison. They've been wild ever since they were enclosed here seven hundred years back. They winna tolerate another cow on that land, nivver mind a man. And dinna think ye can beat them by running. Man, they can move as fast as a race-horse!'

They walked on, Mr Charlton striding ahead, stopping every now and then to scan the park. They went round the edge of the plantation, and began to climb the ridge. Mr Dennison began to puff, and Andrew to think that they would never find the herd; but at last they came upon them. They were all standing on the far side of a patch of straggling gorse. They had stopped grazing, and stood together in a loose group, all facing the intruders, their heads lifted and their horns tilted backwards as they caught the scent of the three watchers. Against the dark green of the gorse their hides glowed, white as snow. They tilted their dark muzzles into the wind, suspicious and alert, but without fear, and still as stones, until one of the bulls moved forward to put himself between the herd and the men.

'Is that the king bull?' asked Mr Dennison.

'Aye, that's him. He's a fine beast, isn't he?'

'He's not quite as handsome as I thought he would be.'

'He's still in his winter coat. He's a bit rough and scruffy, but just wait till he's rubbed that off, Mr Dennison, and then ye'll see what a beauty he is. But he looks to me as if he's been in a fight. Did ye hear the row they were kicking up last night?'

'I did,' said Andrew.

Mr Charlton did not reply. Looking up, Andrew saw his lips moving and his eyes going over the herd as he counted them.

'What's the matter, Uncle?'

'There's a bull missing. Aye, there's been a fight. I had a notion that one of the young 'uns was going to have a go at the king bull. I've seen him shaping up for a battle. What's happened to him, I wonder.'

'Has the king bull killed him?'

'Heaven forfend, hinny. We canna afford to lose a good young bull like him. But he must be hurt or else he'd be with the herd. This is the way they behave, Mr Dennison. When a beast gets hurt he goes off by hissel for a day or two till he gets better. I'll have to find him and see what shape he's in. You'd better go back with Andrew, Mr Dennison. It could take me hours to find him.'

'I'd rather stay with you, if you can put up with me, Warden.'

'So would I, Uncle.'

'Mind, you could be in for a good traipse. You'll feel it afore ye're finished.'

'This is something that doesn't happen every day. I would hate to miss it.'

'It doesn't happen every day, but it happens far ower often for my liking.'

They continued to follow the wall, Mr Charlton striding ahead impatiently, and scanning every hollow where a sick beast might be hiding.

'He'll be up at the top of the fell,' he said. 'It's a funny thing but if one of them's in trouble he always makes for the high ground. Put your best foot forward now. I've got to find him, and find him in a hurry.'

It took them an hour to find the bull, but eventually they spotted him. He had gone into hiding in a little hollow screened by a clump of stunted pines. He was not feeding, but standing facing the wind, his head not raised to the scent, but sagging and hanging forward sickly and mournfully.

'Nae wonder he's gone off by hissel,' said Mr Charlton. 'See what's happened to him?'

'No.'

'He's broken one of his horns. Look, it's hanging loose. That's the end for him, poor beast. If he couldn't beat the king with two horns, he'll never do it with one.'

'Will he get better?'

'He winna peg out, if that's what ye mean. The big question is – will the herd take him back? They dinna like a beast that's blemished in any way.'

'Is there nothing you can do, Warden?'

'Not a thing. These are wild cattle, Mr Dennison. They'll nivver let a mortal man put a finger on them. All ye can do is let the poor beggar come round as best he can. Damn, I thought something like this was happening when I heard them kicking up that row last night. Well, now I know the worst. We'd better get back now and hope for the best.'

But the best did not happen. After a few days the sick bull made an effort to rejoin the herd, but they would not have it. It was driven out and a few days later Mr Charlton found it dead in a bog. The herd had driven it there and kept it in the bog until it had drowned.

Andrew went with his uncle to pull it out and cart it to the butcher's. Before they dared to enter the park, Lord Hetherington had to send one of his grooms, on horseback, and five or six hounds to keep the herd off till the carcase was recovered. The cattle were not afraid of any man, even when

35

mounted, but they had a great fear of being hunted and kept well clear of the hounds.

It was the first time Andrew had been close to one of the wild cattle. The hide was dirty with mud from the bog, but, here and there, where it was clean and the new coat had begun to show through the old, the pelt was white and soft as velvet. The tips of the ears were a fine foxy red, and the muzzle and hooves a glossy black. As the butcher sluiced hot water over it before beginning to cut it up, the beautiful coat shone whiter and purer than ever, and the strong glossy hooves were as black as anthracite.

When the bull had been cut up, most of the meat went to the castle, but, as was the custom, one joint was given to the Warden. It was good meat but Mr Charlton would have nothing to do with it, and gave it to the dog. It took him a few days to get over the loss of the young bull. Night after night he sat glumly staring into the fire, like a man who had lost not only a poor dumb beast but a dear and valued member of his own family.

6

Andy Gets into Trouble

Mr Charlton gave Andrew a few days of freedom before sending him to school, but in the end he had to go. He did not look forward to it, and he did not enjoy it when at last he had to face it. Out of school he could keep clear of Billy Craggs, the boy who had wrestled with him and torn his trousers; but in school there was little chance of avoiding him, and Billy neglected no opportunity to make the new boy's life a misery. He stuck out his foot as Andrew was taking his slate out to the teacher. He filled his inkwell to overflowing and got him into trouble for letting the ink run on to the floor. He rapped at him with his ruler and threw inkballs at him. Nor was there much respite in the playground. There he threw sticky-jacks at Andrew, got boys to hold him down while he chalked KICK ME on the back of his jacket, and slashed at his bare knees with nettles. He taunted Andrew into hitting back at him, then wrestled with him and threw him into dirty puddles.

Andrew had to suffer not only from Billy but also from the schoolmaster. Mr Ridley was a mean man. He was too stupid to command the respect of the boys, but cunning enough to see that he could keep on the side of Billy and his gang by siding with them against the new boy. He made fun of Andrew's handwriting and his way of doing long division, and made him read aloud so that they could all laugh at his accent.

Andrew got through the first few days without disgracing

himself too seriously, but towards the end of the week he found himself in trouble. The castle clock had just struck half past eleven. Mr Ridley called out, 'Put your slates away now, everybody – clean them first. I don't want dirty slates in your desks. And get out your knitting. I don't want a sound from you all before twelve o'clock.'

Andrew thought that he must have made a mistake, but while Mr Ridley began to poke at the fire he saw all the boys and girls take out a ball of wool and a set of needles. He waited for someone to tell Mr Ridley that he had given the wrong order, but no one spoke. They all settled back in their desks while Mr Ridley reached for a dirty frying-pan that hung by the side of the fireplace and set it on the hearth.

Andrew sat looking incredulously around him. He had neither wool nor needles, nor had he any idea of what to do with them if he did possess them. But the boys all round him seemed to know. With astonishing obedience they all clicked away. There was something so comical about the whole performance that Andrew wanted to laugh at it. He felt sure that sooner or later the whole class would burst out laughing and the joke be explained.

But there was no laughter. Instead he saw Mr Ridley looking angrily at him, pointing at him with a fork he had taken from his desk.

'Why aren't you knitting, Robson?'

'I haven't any needles – or wool, sir.'

'Who's away from school today?'

'Billy Turnbull, sir,' said one of the boys.

'Right. Give Robson Billy Turnbull's tackle. You're lucky,' said Mr Ridley. 'But tomorrow, do you understand, you bring your own gear – wool and needles. Now get on with it.'

'I can't, sir.'

'Can't what?'

'I can't get on with it, sir. I don't know how to knit.'

'Did you hear that, boys and girls? Here's a boy – how old are you, Robson?'

'Nearly thirteen, sir.'

'Here's a boy nearly thirteen years of age – and he can't knit, yet.'

To Andrew's surprise the whole class burst out laughing.

'Thirteen years of age – and he doesn't know how to use a pair of needles. Well, we have a proper dummy in school, haven't we?'

It was not often that the class had a chance to laugh. Now it was offered they took it with both hands. They all sat back and laughed, and Mr Ridley's features were creased in an ugly grin.

'Isn't he a beauty, then? What sort of a prize idiot have we got in school now, eh?'

'None of the boys ever knitted in our school, sir,' said Andrew. 'It was just the . . .'

'Be quiet! That's enough back-chat. I don't want to hear what you did in that dirty pit village you came from. You're at Lilburn now, and you'll do what I say you have to do. If you can't knit, you can learn. Pick it up from the boy next door to you. And if you spoil Billy Turnbull's work, I hope he'll give you something that will make you do better next time. Silence everybody – and if you give me any more trouble, Robson, I'll fell you with this frying-pan.'

Andrew took up the needles, but he felt stubborn and angry. If he had to do girls' work, he would do it, but he made up his mind that he would be as awkward as he could, no matter what happened to him.

To his surprise Andrew found that his aunt could see nothing wrong with his having to learn to knit. She quickly found wool and needles for him, and told him that there was nothing effeminate about it. All the men in Lilburn knitted and spent many long hours in the winter knitting special socks and cuffs and mufflers for the bad northern weather. Reluctantly Andrew learnt how to use the needles, and since Mr Ridley never inspected the work that the class was doing but was perfectly happy as long as they were quiet, he kept out of trouble with him in these lessons.

But one day he found himself in serious trouble.

Mr Ridley was a bachelor who lived in a gatehouse at the end of one of the castle drives. This drive was not used very often and the house was neglected. It would have been easy for him to have walked home and taken his midday meal there, but he was greedy and preferred to use the school fire. As soon as it drew near to midday he would give the class some task or other and then set about preparing his dinner. He nearly always had bacon, and while the class was busy reading or knitting he would peel off two or three slices of mouldy bacon and slap them in the pan. Then he would stand with one hand on his cane, and the other on the pan handle, with his eyes on the gate ready for any unexpected caller. All this he did so regularly that for most of the class the smell of frying was as common as all the other smells of the school. The smell set them thinking of their own dinners, and sharpened their appetite for what might be waiting for them at home. Usually Mr Ridley flung open the door as soon as he heard the castle clock strike twelve, and the children ran out in a disorderly mob, but sometimes he would leave the room to fasten the school gate or pay a visit to the closet at the end of the yard.

This afternoon the class reassembled to find him in a great temper. Andrew knew that something had gone wrong with his dinner. Mr Ridley was not a clean eater and often had grease marks on his chin where the bacon fat had run down from his lips. This time his chin was clean.

'Which of you spoilt my dinner when my back was

turned?' he shouted. 'Somebody did it! Somebody came back when I was out and spoilt it. Look at this!'

He held up a slice of bacon. It was covered with what looked like yellow grit.

'Sand!' he yelled. 'Somebody put sand on my dinner! Who was it?'

Nobody spoke.

'I couldn't eat a bite,' he went on. 'Because somebody teemed some sand on my fry. But I'll find out! I won't have anybody tinkering with my meat. Open your desks and put your hands on your heads!'

Andrew lifted the lid of his desk, but what he saw there made him lower it again quickly. In the corner was a crumpled piece of brown paper, and on the bottom of the paper grains of sand. He tried to pull it out and stuff it in his pocket but Mr Ridley saw him.

'What are you trying to hide there – you, Robson? Put your hands on your head!'

He strode over to Andrew's desk and pulled out the paper and shook it. As the grains of sand fell on the floor Andrew knew where it had come from. He had seen a heap of sand like that outside Mr Craggs's greenhouse. But he had no time to explain. Mr Ridley seized him and dragged him out to the front of the class.

'So it was you, was it, you nasty little hoit? I've had my eye on you and your dirty pit ways ever since you came to this school. By God, I'll give you the biggest hugging you've ever had, you little villain. Craggs, come out here and get down!'

Andrew did not know what the master was going to do. At first he thought that Mr Ridley had seen through the trick and was going to punish Craggs first. But he saw Billy come out eagerly, wink at one of the other boys and get down to the floor on all fours. 'You, Reed, and you, Clennel, hold him down for me,' shouted Mr Ridley, rushing to the desk for his cane, and he found himself being thrown on to Billy's back and his arms being pinned round his neck.

'What are you going to do, Mr Ridley?' he asked.

'You'll find out,' the master said, and he began to pull Andrew's trousers down.

When at last Andrew realized what was going to happen to him, the injustice and the humiliation of the punishment made the blood go rushing into his head. Rather than endure this he would hit out, he would draw blood, he would do anything. Before Mr Ridley could get his trousers down he shook himself free of the hold that the other two boys had on him and tightened them round Billy's neck. If he was to suffer, then his enemy would suffer with him. He felt Billy begin to gasp and writhe under his grip.

'He's throppling me, Mr Ridley,' he gasped. 'He's throppling me!'

'I don't care what he's doing,' said Mr Ridley, lifting his cane and tugging at the trousers, but Billy began to buck and twist so violently that he threw Andrew off. Once free, Andrew twisted round and went for the master. The cane came down once on his shoulder, but he did not feel it. Seizing the old man's wrists, he kicked him hard on the shins. At the first kick the master dropped the cane and began to howl, hopping around on his unharmed leg. With one angry push Andrew sent him sprawling into the aisle. Then, picking up the big inkwell from the teacher's desk, he threw the contents over him and ran out of the room.

He did not care what he was doing or where he was running. He ran out of the yard and did not stop till he came to the river half a mile away. He bent down and splashed the cold water over his hands and face as if to wipe off the touch of the nasty old man who had dared to cane him. The cold water calmed him and his anger began to subside. He sat down and began to consider what to do next. His mind was full of notions of flight. He would never go back to school. He would turn his back on the school and the village and everyone in it. He did not know how far he was from Sleetburn, but the distance did not matter. He would begin walking and never stop till he was back home among his own family and his own friends.

But he did not move. Instead he sat on the edge of the burn, watching the water-hens going in and out of the bushes, and the fry making small ripples on the edges of the water. He was still there when Mr Dennison came upon him.

'Hey there,' said the old man. 'Shouldn't you be in school at this time of the day?'

'I've run away.'

'What? You'll have the schoolmaster after you, my boy.'

'But he won't catch me. I'm not going back to his school again.'

'I'm afraid you haven't much say about that, Andrew. The law is not on your side this time. You can't get away with playing truant these days. Something must have happened. Tell me about it.'

Mr Dennison sat down beside Andrew, laying his sketch-book down on the grass. Andrew saw the wind turn over the pages one by one. He told Mr Dennison how he had been unjustly accused, and how Mr Ridley had tried to cane him.

'You mustn't take it too much to heart,' said the old man. 'You mustn't expect everything to be as it was in your old school. Mr Ridley was probably just going to punish you in the way that is customary here. It was probably nothing personal.'

'But I didn't do what he said I'd done, Mr Dennison. He had no proof.'

'Then take my advice. Go quietly back to your uncle, and tell him what you've told me. Let's have no more talk about running away back to Sleetburn. That will do nobody any good. You'll just give your mother more anxiety, and if what you've told me is true she has enough worries. I'll go and see Mr Ridley. And I'll give him a piece of my mind. I haven't been here very long but I've picked up enough about Mr Ridley to know that he's a bit of a silly-billy. We have good allies, Andrew. I'll tell him that if he doesn't run his school on better lines I'll advise Lord Hetherington to dismiss him. I don't think Hetherington will ever bring himself to that, but the threat will put the fear of God into Ridley. Just you go home now – no, on second thoughts it may be better for you to spend the afternoon with me. Go back to your uncle at tea-time and tell him everything that's happened. I'll call tonight and straighten everything out for you. Don't worry. Everything will blow over, you'll see.'

Mr Dennison was as good as his word. Mr Charlton began by being angry with Andrew, but he could not help laughing when he heard how he had kicked Mr Ridley's shin and thrown the ink at him. Then later that night Mr Dennison came to say that he had given the man a good talking to, and scared the life out of him by threatening to have him dismissed if he did not deal more justly with his pupils. When Andrew went to bed that night he felt that he had done two good things. With the help of Mr Dennison he had taught the stupid Mr Ridley that he was not to be made a fool of. The second thing pleased him even more. He had begun – without the aid of Mr Dennison – to settle scores with Billy Craggs. He remembered how he had made him squeal with the strength of his grip. He began to think that Billy was maybe not as strong as he made himself out to be. For the first time Andrew began to realize that if only he could learn to wrestle he might be able to hold his own against Billy or anybody else in Lilburn.

7

The Fox

'Are ye ready up there then, Andy?' called his uncle. He was down in the peat bog. It was his own 'hag' as he called it. Nobody else was allowed to cut peat from it, and for as long as anyone could remember it had been called the Warden's Hag.

'What do you want me to do with the peats, Uncle?' asked Andrew.

'Just spread them out on the ground.'

'Anywhere?'

'Aye, anywhere, so lang as they dinna touch. I want them to get dry on the top side.'

He put his foot on his long-handled shovel, cut a peat from the black, sticky bog, then threw it up over his shoulder. It was warm down in the hag and his hair was sticking to his scalp. At first Andrew did not know what to expect, and the peats kept hitting him as he turned his back and bent down to spread them. He hoped his uncle would not see how badly he was doing the job. In the last few weeks Andrew had vexed him by doing a dozen silly things. He had forgotten over and over again to clean the gardening tools after he had done with them, and once left a saw out in the rain. He had been asked to do a bit of sowing and had put the seeds in the wrong distance apart and his uncle had to do it again. He was ashamed of being such a duffer, and anxious to make a good job of helping with the peats. Fortunately, his uncle could not see the mistakes he was making. On the contrary, he was grateful for help.

'It's great weather for the peats,' he said, stopping and wiping his brow with his forearm. 'Are ye managing all right up there?'

'Yes, Uncle.'

'They'll not be lang in drying in this wind.'

The wind was not strong, but, up above, the big white clouds moved like galleons. Andrew watched them billow up over the line of the hills, swelling and rising, then launching themselves into the wide sky. There was no snow now on Cheviot, and it lay humped on the far skyline, like a blue leviathan. The sheep were feeding on the fell, moving steadily over the hill, the lambs lagging behind them, then catching up with a run and dabbing viciously at the udders of the ewes. They were too big now to be sucking and the ewes pushed them off. Little grey birds went from tussock to tussock, springing into the air and letting the wind carry them to the next clump of heather: and the upper air was filled with the sound of curlews as they wheeled and circled.

After a while Mr Charlton came out for a rest.

'I'm rozzelled in there,' he said. 'I'll have to come out for a minute or else I'll be roastit.'

They sat down on the heather and let the wind cool them. From this shank of hill they could not see the park, but before them was the hill where the shepherd ran his flock, and beyond it the other hags where the villagers cut their peats. While they were sitting resting, they saw a man with a sack over his shoulder coming up the fell towards them.

'This is the lad I was telling you about the other night,' said Mr Charlton. 'Ye wouldn' take him for a champion wrestler, would you?'

Andrew watched the man loping easily over the fell. He was rather spare in build, with a lean bony face. There was a

46

queer whiteness on the bridge of his nose as if the skin was stretched too tightly over it, but he had a light, springy walk that carried him nimbly over the slope.

'Are ye walking the hill, Dickie?' asked Mr Charlton as he came up to them.

'Aye. We've got a big fox somewhere up here,' he said. 'He's a gay big yin and he's ower wick for the dogs to get him, but I keep coming up to see if I can frighten him off. He's had one or two lambs already. He's somewhere about here. Can ye hear him?'

They looked out over the hill. Andrew could not see anything but he could hear the grouse calling 'G'back, g'back, g'back', as they always did when they were disturbed.

'He's after a few eggs or chicks. Dod, he's a greedy beggar. He'll eat anything he can come by. If he comes a bit closer, I'll set the dogs on him.'

At that moment they saw the fox come out of the heather. It was nosing its way from clump to clump, stopping every now and then to snack at something. 'Go on, Beattie, go on. Spot! Fetch him, fetch him!' said the shepherd, and the two dogs went racing across the shank.

'They'll catch up with him, but they'll never get a grip on him. Their teeth are not sharp enough for that sort of game. But they'll give him a run for his money, and mebbe mek him think twice of coming round here again.'

A few minutes later the dogs came back. They threw themselves on the ground, their sides going up and down like a bellows and their tongues lolling inches long out of their mouths.

'Do you think they got him, Mr Ingram?' asked Andrew.

'No,' he said. He put his hand in Spot's mouth and pulled the loose flesh back from his gums. 'Not a trace of blood. But mebbe they've warned him off for a few days.'

47

He whistled up his dogs, threw his sack over his shoulder and went off.

'He's very thin for a wrestler, isn't he, Uncle Adam?' said Andrew.

'Aye, but ye cannot judge everything by the outside. He's a spelk of a lad, but he can get the better of most of the big fellers.'

Andrew watched the shepherd loping away over the fell. Now that he had seen what a good wrestler looked like he felt cheered. If Dickie with his slight frame could beat all the big men in Lilburn perhaps he could learn to get the better of fat Billy Craggs.

There was another heartening consequence to the day. His uncle was pleased with the help he had given him with the peats, and let him go up to the hag a few days later to get on by himself. It wasn't much of a job. All he had to do was to lean the turfs together two by two with the dry side underneath.

He went carefully over the ground, fitting the peats together. His back did not ache now as it had done when he started helping his uncle, and he liked setting the peats up like little roofs; but while he was working he heard something disturbing the grouse again on the hillside opposite. He straightened his back, and, shading his eyes, he made out the shape of the fox. It was raiding the hillside again, nosing its way among the gorse and heather, stopping every now and then to feed on something, eggs or young birds, perhaps even a sitting bird that refused to leave the nest. The dogs had not scared it away. It must have known it had nothing to fear from them.

When he had first seen the fox Andrew had been excited. It was the first time he had seen one at close quarters. But now he hated it. He wished he had been able to bring Cappy with him, but his uncle still did not like it to be loose. He began to wonder if the fox would get over the park wall and trouble the herd. He had heard his uncle say that the cattle did not like a fox and would stampede if one ran among them. He yelled at it and threw stones, but it took no notice of him and went on padding from hollow to hollow, indifferent and greedy.

⌒8⌒

Tickling Trout

As day followed day, Andrew grew more used to living in
Lilburn. He began to learn how to fit in with his uncle's ways,
how to avoid giving too much offence to Mr Ridley, and, best
of all, how to get the measure of the obnoxious Billy Craggs.
He kept his eye on him in the playground and noticed that
though he was strong he was easily puffed. When the boys
were playing some energetic game in the yard, such as Tiggy
or Tally-ho, he was always the first to give up and take a rest.
Andrew noticed that he would often fall out of the game and
rest with his back up against the school wall, puffing and
blowing. When he got his wind back he would join in the
game again and use his strength and cunning to give some
smaller boy a nasty toss. The way to avoid being hurt by him
was to keep him running and never get within reach of his
powerful arms.

Although after the affair of Mr Ridley's dinner the boys
took fewer liberties with Andrew, none had yet come over to
his side. Billy was still the king of the schoolyard, and most of
the boys were too afraid of him and of Mr Ridley to desert
him. But there was one boy who began to play with Andrew,
a slip of a boy called Alec Cowen, with a thin face and straight
fair hair almost as soft as a girl's. The upper part of his cheeks
was sunburnt and freckled, but the skin under his eyes was
white, almost transparent, and he had a redness on the side of
his chin, as if he had grazed it and the scrape would not heal.

He had thin legs and bony white knees, but he was not a weakling. He could trot like a horse, throwing his knees higher than anyone else in the class, and he could cartwheel across the grass at great speed. Of all the boys in the school he was the least afraid of Billy, and Billy did not like him because he could not catch him. It was Alec who taught Andrew how to outwit Billy, and it was their success in taunting and angering him that brought them together.

Even then Andrew's ignorance of country ways made Alec impatient with him at times. His head was stuffed with colliery matters. He knew all about hewing coal and filling it and screening it, but he knew next to nothing about birds and beasts and fishes.

One day Alec took him down to the burn to tickle trout, and he almost spoilt the sport from the word go by rushing up to the edge of the pool as if he had never seen water before.

'Hey, dinna gan clumping up like that!' said Alec. 'Ye'll frighten all the fish away, and they'll nivver come back as lang as they can hear you thumping the ground. Just come up to the edge of the bank quietly, and try not to cast a shadow on the watter. Look, there's a big yin! Keep an eye on him and see which hag he gans under.'

'What's a hag?'

'It's that bit of the bank that hangs over the burn. Look – he's seen us and he's off. Under that hag! Keep an eye on him.'

He walked quietly upstream, leapt across the burn, and came cautiously down the other side.

'Is he still there?'

'Aye.'

'Under this hag?'

'Aye.'

'Keep still then, and I'll pull him oot.'

He lay down on the grass with only his head, arms and

shoulders hanging over the water. He rolled up his sleeve and slid his arm, very quietly, down into the water and in under the hag.

'I can feel him,' he whispered. 'I'm touching him. Keep still till I lift him oot.'

For a full minute Alec kept his hand under the water. Then suddenly he pulled it out and flung the trout on to the bank. It twisted and bent itself backwards and forwards to get back into the water, but Alec got both his hands on it. Thrusting a thumb into its mouth he pressed its head back until the gills broke. Andrew could hear them cracking like small bones. Then the fish lay still.

'Can I try it?' asked Andrew. He was greatly impressed by Alec's skill. He had never known that you could catch a fish without rod and line.

'Anybody can try it, but watch out for the water bailiff. Want to try now?'

'Yes.'

'Just wait quietly, then, till the fish come out again.'

They lay down on the bank and waited till the fish began to venture out into the pool again.

'There's a big yin,' said Alec. 'Have a go at him. Keep your eye on him. As soon as he gets wind we're after him he'll get under a hag. There he is. Put your hand in there.'

Andrew lay down and began to slide his hand into the water. It was very cold but it was not the coldness that put him off. He didn't like the idea of putting his arms into the cold, secret darkness of the hag.

'What if there's a rat under there?' he asked apprehensively.

'Dinna be so flayed, man. There's nowt there that will bite ye. Put your hand in till ye touch the fish, then get your hand right round it afore ye pull.'

'Will it let me touch it?'

52

'Aye, if you're not clumsy and noisy. Can you feel it?'

'Yes.'

'Stroke it, then.'

To Andrew's astonishment, the fish let him touch its flank. He passed his fingers slowly down its side, feeling the open fin, the scaly side and then the soft underbelly.

'How do you get hold of it?' he whispered.

'Grip it round the thick part.'

'Now?'

'Dinna grab till ye've got a good grip.'

Andrew waited till he could feel both thumb and finger touching the fish, then he grabbed wildly. The fish shot out of his hand and darted away across the pool.

'I've missed it,' he cried.

'No, ye haven' got the knack,' said Alec. 'You're far ower rough and clumsy. Ye'll nivver catch one here now that ye've let that big yin off.'

'Can I try somewhere else?'

'Ye can try farther up the burn, but it's not so good there.'

They tried again and again, but Andrew could not manage to hold his fish. He could get his hand to them, but he could not get one out of the water. In the end they gave up and went off to do something else. Andrew was ashamed of himself. He felt a duffer, ignorant and clumsy. Alec, too, seemed to lose interest in him, and did not take him fishing again.

9

The Park Warden

Mr Dennison took to coming more and more frequently to the Warden's cottage.

'It may sound strange, Andrew,' he said, 'but I'd rather be here than up at the castle. I would rather hear your uncle talking about his herd than Lord George blathering about his horses and dogs. And he doesn't think you're a man if you don't drink yourself silly every night. I shall be glad to get back to my studio for a few days.'

'Are you going away?'

'Just for a week or so. I've done all my sketches, and I'm going back to do the full canvases in my studio. Any news from your home, Andrew? That place with the harsh name.'

'Sleetburn?'

'That's it. It makes me cold every time I hear it. Any news about your father?'

'Not yet, Mr Dennison.'

'I'll tell you what, Andrew, if I have the time I'll call and see for myself how your mother is getting on. Then when I come back I'll have some first-hand news for you. But first of all I have a few drawings for you to look at. What do you think of these?'

'That's the king bull!'

'Yes, that's him, in his scruffy winter coat. He doesn't look quite as fierce as he does in *The History of Quadrupeds*, does he? But the old man who wrote that book wasn't as cautious

54

as we are. He tried to get close one day, and the bull treed him. Perhaps that's why he made him look so fierce. Now look at this one.'

'That's the young bull that was drowned.'

'Your uncle was very cut up about that, wasn't he? He really loves that herd. But I'll tell you why I've brought these drawings. I want you to keep them, Andrew, till I get back. I daren't leave them up at the castle. Hetherington is such a fool at times that he would think nothing of lighting his pipe with them.'

Mr Charlton put the pictures away in his desk and the two men sat down to talk about the cattle. No one knew more about them than Andrew's uncle. The Charltons had been Park Warden for many generations, and the present warden had taken care to store up in his mind as much as was known about them. He knew about the first enclosing of the herd in the thirteenth century, and he himself kept in the desk the first written records of its numbers. He liked to speak with Mr Dennison about the way in which the herd had survived since its first enclosure without the introduction of new stock, about the strange custom that the cattle had of electing a king bull that had to defend his title against all rivals by his strength and skill in fighting, about their mistrust of human beings, about their mysterious immunity from all the diseases that ordinary cattle suffered from. But one thing always troubled him – his concern about the thoughtlessness of Lord George, who did not seem to understand how rare the cattle were, but hunted down the young bulls whenever some silly guest took a fancy to that kind of sport.

'We've always – I mean us Wardens – we've always looked on it as a matter of pride to keep the herd in good fettle. I remember my father and his father before him. When a new calf was dropped, it was as good as a holiday to them; but when they lost one of the herd it was a black day for everybody. Ye may not credit it, but my grandfather used to go into black whenever he lost one of his cattle. Folks used to laugh at him and think he was a bit queer, but that didn't stop him. He used to go into mourning just as if it was somebody in the family that had died.'

'And what's going to happen when you get too old for the job, Mr Charlton?'

'I try not to think about that. If I'd had a son I would have trained him as my father trained me. But God hasn't seen fit to send us any bairns, and I doubt if we'll have any family now. I just keep on hoping that some young feller will come on the scene one of these days. One thing's certain. I'll nivver get any peace till I've found somebody that will look after the herd the way the Charltons have done.'

'And what about Hetherington's son? Does he show any interest in the cattle?'

'Ah now, there's something that makes me feel a bit mair hopeful about the future. I haven't seen much of him. They say he's still away at college somewhere, but he strikes me as having mair brains in his little finger than the old feller has in his head. He'll be a good laird, and if he's lucky enough to get a good warden as weel, the cattle might see better days than they have for many years.'

Andrew sat on his cracket knitting and listening to the men. Often at home he had sat listening to his father and his marras talking about their pit-work, about shifts and prices, the kind of coal they were hewing, and the prospects of getting a new and easier place. Now the talk was all about bulls and heifers, calves and pasture, the perils of foxes and severe winters. It was more interesting than pit-talk, and Andrew found himself wishing that he had been his uncle's son, so that he could have grown up to be the next Park Warden and the keeper of those parchments that his uncle kept in his desk.

56

∽10∾

New Boots for Andy

All this while he had had no news from home. This did not trouble him too much. He had begun to get over his homesickness, and he knew that his mother and his brother, who had started work in the pit, were not fond of writing letters. 'Anyhow,' his aunt kept saying, 'no news is good news, and your mother has enough on her plate without having to put pen to paper.'

But one day a letter came from Mr Barnes.

Dear Andrew,

Just a few lines hoping this finds you in the pink as it leaves me at present. The news about your father is that his legs are on the mend, thank God, but he hasn't been discharged yet from the Infirmary. So your mother wants me to say that if you are enjoying yourself with your Aunt Florrie and you can keep on at Lilburn you have not to think of coming home yet. Your Nat has started as a putter now and that means a bit more coming in every week. Say thanks to your Aunt Florrie for the butter and ham that she sent. You know that your mother does not like writing, but I'm only too pleased to do it for her. The neighbours have all been tiptop and she is managing very nicely. Drop her a line now and then. One of the horses went lame last week and that put me in a bit of a pickle, but he's on the mend now and I'll be starting carrying the coals again next week. It will be a bit afore your father gets out of the Infirmary, but come Christmas he should be back to normal. There's not much news here except that the men from the B. Pit have been idle for a few days but things are picking up and the management has plenty orders now. We have a new minister at the chapel but he's not a patch on the old one. He's a bit on the prim and proper side, and likes to take a bit too much into his own hands. I cannot think of any more news so I'll finish now with best wishes from the family and from

Yours sincerely,

John Barnes

'Well now, I must say that it's nice of him to write. He's a good friend to the family, and you'd better sit down tonight and drop him a line.'

'Aye, he writes a good letter,' said Mr Charlton, 'but it looks as if ye'll be with us for a bit yet, Andy. Well, you're welcome, hinny. Ye can bide here as long as your mother wants ye to. I'm sure we all enjoy your company. Would ye like to stop here?'

'Yes, Uncle.'

'Are ye happy in the school now?'

'I don't like Mr Ridley.'

'Does he still pick on you?'

'A little bit, but I'm not frightened of him.'

'And what about the lads? Do they still fight with you?'

'Sometimes. But Alec plays with me.'

'Ye'll have to be patient with them, hinny. They're queer folk here in Lilburn. They're a bit like the cattle. They dinna take very easily to strangers.'

When Andrew sat down to write to Mr Barnes he did not tell him how homesick he had been, partly because he did not

58

want his mother to think he was unhappy, and partly because he was already beginning to feel that he belonged to Lilburn as much as to Sleetburn. Alec had begun to play with him again, and from him he had begun to pick up the language of the village, the words they used for the birds and beasts and fishes and flowers. He had begun to fall into Lilburn ways. He was no longer surprised to see his uncle throwing his stockings in the oven when he went to bed, he never noticed the smell of the peat-fires, and often, on wet nights, he would find himself picking up his needles and getting on with his knitting.

One night when he was lying in bed he heard his uncle and his aunt talking about him. It was still light and he had left his bedroom door open so that he could read a few pages before he went to sleep. He was not reading so much as looking at the illustrations in *The History of Quadrupeds*.

'I dinna think much of these boots that Andrew fetched with him,' he heard his aunt say. 'Just brown paper if ye ask me. And look at his stockings. Every day they're as wet as a clout. These boots winna stand up to the bad weather when it comes.'

'Get him fitted up wi' a new pair, Florrie. Get Simey the cobbler to knock him up a decent pair for the winter.'

'I think I will. These are shoddy affairs. And there's another thing I dinna like very much – that thing that he wears around his neck on weekdays. Nae wonder the lads med fun of him.'

'All the lads in the collieries wear things like that. I've seen them.'

'It may be all right in the colliery, but I think it's out of place here. I'd like him to wear a proper necktie.'

So Andrew had to give up the collier's necktie, with the knot at the side, that he had brought with him from Sleetburn, and to exchange his flimsy boots for the new pair that the cobbler made for him. At first he thought he would never be able to wear them. Like all the workmen's boots they had upturned soles, and Andrew could hardly get his feet into them. But after a while his feet did not ache so much. They did not get wet so often now, and he didn't catch cold so easily. A few weeks ago anyone looking into the playground would have picked him out as an obvious stranger. Now no one could tell the difference between him and the boys who had lived in Lilburn all their lives.

∽11∽

The New Calf

On several occasions when he was at the peats Andrew saw the fox. He heard Dickie complaining that it had got one or two more of his lambs, and saying that if he had not already been in Hetherington's bad books he would have taken a gun to it; but Lord George was very keen on hunting and would never forgive anyone for meddling with the foxes. Dickie kept driving it away and told Andrew that the next best thing to setting the dogs on it was to get a good catapult. So Andrew got a length of strong rubber from a pedlar who came round one day and made himself a catapult that was capable of shooting a fair-sized stone a hundred yards. His uncle encouraged him to use it for he did not like the idea of the fox getting into the park and bothering the herd. 'He's a cheeky beggar,' he said, 'and I've known foxes like him take a calf before now.'

Andrew spent a lot of his free time on the hill and near the park, and one day during the Whitsuntide holidays he went out with his catapult to look at the herd. His uncle told him he was hoping for a calf, but he never knew for certain when to expect one. The white cattle were so unusually built that you could never tell for certain when they were in calf.

He could see the herd on the far side of the park and was preparing himself for a long walk when he saw something moving in a thicket not far from the wall. It was the ears of one of the cattle, and he could tell from the shape of the horns that it was a heifer, for they were turned backwards and inwards. He knew enough about the herd to realize that the heifer had withdrawn from the herd because she was hurt, or ready to drop her calf, or was suckling one that she had already dropped. He was determined to find out and kept his place by the wall until at last he saw the horns move, and the heifer turned round and began to make her way back to the herd. He was certain now that she had calved. He could see no blemish on her, and she was making her way across the park confidently. But he did not dare to get over the wall and make sure. His uncle had told him that if a heifer suspected that a human being had been near her calf she would destroy it.

He stayed until the heifer had moved out of sight, then got up, thinking he had better go and tell his uncle what he had seen; but just as he was about to go he saw something else moving in the plantation beyond the thicket. It was the fox. It was padding hungrily through the bracken. He saw it sniff here and there, then suddenly stop and lift its muzzle as if it had caught a new scent. Andrew knew what had happened. It had caught the scent of the calf.

It was the same old dog fox that he had seen bothering the ewes on the hill, a cunning beast with a strong, greedy muzzle and a big black brush. A new-born calf would have little chance against those hungry jaws. Long before the heifer could get back to it, it would be dead.

Andrew reached for his catapult. He had a few pebbles in his pocket but he decided to keep them in reserve, and begin with the pieces of stone that had fallen from the wall. He fired his first shot, but the stone fell a score of yards short of the fox. It looked up and stood still for a few seconds, but, knowing that there was little danger, it began to pad forward closer and closer to the edge of the thicket.

Andrew knew that if he was to save the calf he would have

to get nearer. He was not sure now where the herd was for it had moved out of sight, and the heifer with it. It might be close enough to attack, but it did not seem near enough to prevent the fox from making a kill. Once it had killed it could bide its time and come back to devour the carcase at its leisure. There was nothing for Andrew to do but take a risk, to get over the wall and come close enough to score a hit. He quietly filled both pockets with stones, slid silently over the wall, and began to crawl through the grass.

By now the fox was sure of the scent of the calf and was making greedily for the form in which it lay. It had sunk its wet muzzle low and forward, and was sniffing hungrily. Fortunately Andrew was downwind of it, but he knew that he would have to move smartly. Besides, it would not be enough to scare the fox away. He had seen it come back to the hill time and time again after the dogs had driven it away. He would have to hurt it and hurt it so badly that it would think twice of coming back. Fortunately at that moment the fox turned sideways to him and gave him a perfect target. He took the sharpest stone he could find and let fly. It was a good shot. It struck the fox on the upper part of its back leg. It jumped as if shot by a gun, and ran off back to the plantation. He sent another two shots after it and one of them seemed to graze its head. It was running on three legs, and when it got to the plantation it stopped to toss its head and give a lick at its leg. Then it went off again with the injured leg lifted clear of the ground.

Then Andrew heard the pounding of hooves and knew that the heifer had been alarmed and was coming for him. He had just time to get back on the safe side of the wall before the heifer appeared.

The heifer entered the thicket and he could see its horns rising and falling as it bent down to reassure itself that the calf was safe; but Andrew knew that sooner or later it would return to the herd and the calf would be left unprotected again. He knew that it would be dangerous to leave his post now. The fox had been hurt, but it was a bold and cunning animal, and if it was hungry enough it would come back. So all through the afternoon and well into the evening he kept watch over the invisible calf. He did not know what his aunt would say at his failure to turn up for his meals, but he did not care. He had to keep watch. His uncle had set his heart on getting a new calf and would never forgive him if he let the fox get it. At last, when the long summer's day was coming to an end he saw the heifer come back once more to its calf. Listening carefully he heard it bed down beside the calf in the bracken. Then he knew he could relax his watch and go home.

'Mercy on us, lad,' said his aunt when he went in, 'where on earth have you been all day? You've had us all flayed out of our wits wondering what had become of you. Where have ye been?'

'Is my uncle in, Aunt Florrie?'

'He's out at the back, working on the peat stack. But –'

'I have to tell him something,' said Andrew, running out.

His uncle was loading peats onto the stack, and getting ready to put a thatch of heather on it.

'So you've turned up, then? You've had your aunt worried to death.'

'Uncle, I think one of the heifers has calved.'

'What?'

'And there's a fox after it.'

'Did he get it?'

'I don't think so. I haven't seen the calf but I'm sure it's there. I got a shot in at the fox and he nipped off.'

'Ye've not been firing a gun, have ye?'

'No, I used a catapult.'

'And ye've been up there all day – wi'out a bite to eat?'

64

'Yes.'

'Well, I must say ye've done a grand day's work, Andy. Has the heifer bedded down wi' the calf?'

'Yes.'

'Then it will be safe for the night – but ye'll be famished, aren't ye?'

'I'm hungry.'

'I bet ye are. Come in, bonny lad, and fill thy belly. Where's the calf, then?'

'In the big thicket fornenst the plantation.'

'I'll be up there first thing in the morning. But away in and get your supper. Ye've earned it.'

'Mind,' said his aunt when they went into the kitchen, 'I hope you're not going to make a practice of coming in at all hours of the day and expecting to find something on the table . . .' But her husband did not let her finish.

'Nay, dinna get on to the lad, Florrie,' he said. 'He's done a bonny good job of work for us all today. We've got a calf, Florrie. But if it hadn't ha been for Andy there would not have been much of it left by now.'

Mr Charlton was up at first light the next day. He had been up to the park and back by the time Andrew was up.

'Well, the calf's safe, Andy,' he said, when they met at breakfast. 'It's a heifer calf and it's on its own two feet. It's a strong little beggar and the fox will think twice now of having a go at it. In a day or two the heifer will fetch it out and let the herd have a look at it. Ye'd better come out wi' me for the next few days and see what happens. It's worth watching, Andy.'

For the next few days Mr Charlton kept in close touch with the herd, and whenever he went to the park he took Andrew with him. On the third day they saw the heifer go into the covert and lead the calf out. It looked small, smaller than an ordinary calf, but it was strong and very steady on its legs. Its

coat was a beautiful pure white. Its ears had not yet begun to
redden, but its delicate little hooves were already a deep
glossy black.

'Watch this, Andy. This is a ticklish few minutes.'

'Why?'

'They're going to inspect the new calf. If it's a good yin the
herd will accept it. If it isn't, it might just as well never ha'
been born.'

'What will they do?'

'They'll drive it away. Not even its own mother will have
anything to do with it.'

'You mean they'll let it die?'

'They might even kill it themsels. If it isn't up to scratch
the fox can have it for all they care. Keep watching, and you'll
know what they've decided in a few minutes.'

Very quietly, strangely indifferent to the calf that trotted
after it, the heifer walked towards the herd. The cattle all
turned towards her and the calf, but with the same indiffer-
ence and aloofness. The calf stopped as if it already knew
what to do, and for what seemed to Andrew an interminable
time the herd stood stock-still, keeping their distance, looking at the calf, but making no effort either to welcome or repel
it. Then, very slowly and deliberately, the king bull walked
up to the calf and bent forward to sniff it. The calf stood
perfectly still as if it understood the ritual and knew what was
expected of it, while the bull began to walk right round it,
smelling its flanks, its legs, its shoulders and head.

'He's the one that really matters, Andy,' whispered Mr
Charlton. 'If he's satisfied the rest will be. What's he going to
say – yes or no?'

Very slowly the bull went in full circle round the calf. It
bent down once more to sniff at its muzzle, then turned away
and walked with the same air of aloofness back to the herd.

'I think he said yes,' said Andrew.

'So do I, but it's not all over yet. Watch the rest.'

After the king bull it was the turn of all the heifers to inspect the newcomer, and after them the young bulls. One by one they plodded up and went through the ritual. Only when they had all finished did the calf relax. It sat down on the ground, curled its legs under it, and prepared to sleep.

Then the whole herd began to move as if some spell had been removed. They moved their heads and began to swing their tails. The heifers went off to graze, and the bulls began to rub themselves against the trunks of old trees. Neither bulls nor heifers displayed any warmth or welcome towards the calf. It had been accepted, but it was still the youngest and weakest member of the herd. None of the beasts, not even its mother, fussed over it or went out of its way to show any special concern for it. It went to its mother to be suckled, but once it had fed, it withdrew again and took its rightful place, apart from the herd, unaccompanied and inferior.

12

The Sheep Dipping

Although Andrew often saw Mr Ingram, he had not yet dared to broach the subject of wrestling to him. Dickie lived with his father and mother in a very ramshackle cottage high up on the side of Makendon Fell. Andrew and Alec often called there. It was lonely up on the fell and old Mrs Ingram loved visitors. Now that he had given up shepherding the old man had put on weight and looked plump, but his wife was a lean little woman who seemed to have shrunk so much that everything was now too big for her – the wedding ring on her finger, the big sloppy shoes, even the big false teeth that clicked and clattered as she spoke. But they were both very jolly and fond of music. The old man was a piper, not a Scottish bagpiper but a Northumbrian piper, with a set of small-pipes that he did not blow into but filled with a bellows under one arm. As a young man he had been the hereditary piper to the Duke of Northumberland. At the beginning of every recital he played a simple tune called Chevy Chase; when he played it the second time you knew that the concert was over. Sometimes his wife would sing ballads to his accompaniment. Her voice was very sweet for an old woman, and no matter how long the song was she did not forget a word.

Old Mr Ingram was a great story-teller, and he told the boys many a strange tale about the famous border country where he had spent the whole of his long life. One night he told them of a strange discovery he had made many years ago when he was cutting peats. At the bottom of the hag his spade struck against something hard, and when he dug it out he found it was a coffin, and in the coffin, perfectly preserved was the body of a soldier.

'Dod,' he said, 'I had the fright of my life when I took the lid off and saw that young feller there in his blue trousers and his red coat. He must ha' been buried for scores of years, but he looked as fresh as if he was asleep, not dead and buried. We buried him properly in the churchyard, but just afore we put him in I cut all the silver buttons off his jacket. I've given most of them away, one time or another, for keepsakes, but I still keep one. Just pass me that tin, Andrew, will ye?'

'Did you find out who it was, Mr Ingram?'

'No. The minister said he must have been a young officer killed in the time when the Scots and the English were always having a go at one another here. But I'll nivver forget the day when I saw that lad with his fair hair staring up at me out of the bottom of the hag.'

For some days after this Andrew went from hag to hag searching for wooden coffins sticking out of the peat, but he never found one.

The story that made them all laugh was the story of Mr Ingram's visit to Edinburgh.

'I was working on the other side of the border then, at a place called Soutra Mains, and one day the master persuaded me to ga' wi' him to a tup sale in Leith, and when we finished he wouldn't come back wi'oot taking me to Edinburgh for something to eat. So off we went to a muckle big shop, him dodging first through yan door and then another, and me doddlin' after him like a little dog. Why, in the finish he oppened one door, and we went into what looked like a verra little room wi' naebody in but a young woman. He stoppit in this room and sae did I, expecting him to open anither door – when, oot, up she went, the whole room, like a rocket. Dod, I

69

thought, it's an earthquake, and I let oot a yell that flayed that young woman out of her wits.'

'It was a lift,' said Andrew.

'Aye, it was a lift, but how, in the name of heaven, was a poor shepherd like me to ken that? I nivver knew sic a thing existed. It was twelvemonth after the maister stopped pulling my leg about that.'

Andrew had never known anyone as happy as these two old folk with their music and their stories. The old man even made a joke out of the tumbledown ruin that they shared with the cows and poultry and pigs on the top of the fell.

'It's a gay bad hoose, Andy,' he would say, 'but naebody can look doon on us, can they?'

Lord George, who was stingy with his workmen, allowed only one horse between the Park Warden and the shepherd, and Andrew often went backwards and forwards between the two houses, fetching or returning the horse. One day he went to fetch it for his uncle who had been told to bring some timber down from the park; he found old Mr Ingram and his son in the byre looking at a litter of pups that one of the sheep-dogs had just given birth to.

'It's a gay fine litter,' said Dickie, 'but it's put me in a bit of a pickle. I've just fixed up to tak the flock to be dipped the morn, and I dinna like the notion of taking the bitch from her pups for a whole day.'

'Would you like me to help you?' asked Andrew.

'I wadden' say no, Andy. Can ye get away tomorrow?'

'It's Saturday.'

'So it is.'

'Should I bring Cappy?'

'Not on your life. He's useless wi' the flock. He'll be worse than useless. But it will be a long tiring day for ye, Andy.'

'I don't care.'

'Ye'll feel it afore ye're finished.'

'Let the lad come, Dickie,' said Mr Ingram. 'Ye'll have your work cut out wi' just the one dog.'

'I'd welcome a bit of help. What do you say, Mother? Can ye put something up for the lad to eat?'

'Nae trouble at all. If he's good enough to help ye, I'll see that he dissent gan hungry.'

The next day Andrew got up with his uncle, who was always an early riser, but even then when he had got to the cottage Dickie had begun on the day's work and brought the flock down from the hill. They were very restless and seemed to know what was in store for them. Dickie had driven them all into the two big stells outside the cottage and barred the openings with hurdles. But the sheep were nervous and kept up a continuous bleating, and some of the young ewes kept trying to scramble over the stone wall of the stells. As soon as Dickie let them out they began to stream back up the hill and the single dog had a hard time heading them off.

'They know they're gannen to be dipped and they mortally hate it,' said Dickie. 'We'll have a tough job getting them there.'

There was only one dipping place in Lilburn and all the shepherds in the area used it. It stood in a hollow about a couple of miles out of the village.

'We'll have to drive the beggars every inch of the way,' said Dickie. 'Cut yourself a stick, and keep on the far side. Dinna shout and rave at them, but dinna let them break away. They'll be away back to the hill afore ye can say Jack Robinson if ye give them half a chance.'

They headed the flock away from the stells and began to drive them along the track. The way was narrow, but the ground on either side was open and easy to cover. Dickie took the left flank, and used the dog to cover the rear. It was Andrew's job to keep the right flank from breaking.

At first the flock gave them little trouble, but it was a hot

71

day and the flies came off the bracken and hung like a cloud over the sweating sheep. When Andrew got near to the flock they buzzed round him and settled on his face and hands. He hated the feel of the flies on his flesh and kept drawing away from the sheep to get rid of them.

Then as they topped the first rise the flock began to rebel.

'They can smell the dip,' said Dickie. 'Watch them auld ewes. They know what they're in for and they'll turn back if we dinna watch them.'

It was not easy to keep them moving now in the right direction. The dog kept running backwards and forwards at the tail of the flock snapping at the heels of the stragglers. Dickie kept waving his hand and calling 'Hoo, hoo, hoo!' The air was filled with the continuous bleating of the animals, a bewildered and fearful complaint. Andrew did not dare to take his eyes off them, but went quickly backwards and forwards till he began to sweat with the exertion. As they got over the rise and the ground became rougher it was all he could do to stop himself from stumbling. Then one of the ewes made a break. He went for it, put his foot in a hole and went sprawling and lost his stick. By the time he had picked himself up he saw that half a dozen old ewes had broken away and were scurrying back.

'What the devil are ye up to, lad?' shouted Dickie. 'Keep an eye on them, man! Head them off!'

But Andrew was too slow to catch up with the ewes. He stopped helplessly, looking to Dickie for instructions.

'Damn,' said Dickie. 'What were ye doing to let them get away like that?'

'I fell down.'

'For God's sake, keep on thy feet. If tha's given a job, do it!'

It was a difficult job to round up the stragglers, and when it was done the dog was almost exhausted. Its tail was between

72

its legs and his head dropped forward. 'If ye keep on doing that, Andy, ye'll be mair of a hindrance than a help.'

Andrew could see that he was vexed, and he was ashamed of himself for being so stupid. He wondered how he could ask Dickie to help him when he had been such a fool over the first little job that had been given him.

Fortunately the sheep, as if disheartened by the failure of their rebellion, seemed at last ready to submit to their fate, and allowed themselves to be penned in the enclosures that stood around the dipping pond.

It was close and airless down by the pond. The water, yellow and scummy with dip, gave off an acrid smell. In their fear the sheep urinated and dropped their excrement on the floor of the enclosures, and in their restlessness trod it into a smelly mess; and the flies continued to buzz and swarm around every living thing. Andrew's job was to move the flock in small groups from the enclosures into the small pen opening on to the pool, where Dickie stood with a big waterproof apron tied round his middle. The small ewes and the lambs were easy to handle but the old ewes were heavy and mutinous. Andrew got them by the horns but they pulled obstinately away from him. It was not long before his arms began to ache with the strain, but he did not dare to stop till they had dipped half the flock and Dickie said it was time to eat. By that time he was so tired he could hardly speak, and could hardly force the food down his dry throat.

It was well after five when they finished. By then Andrew was so tired that he thought he would never be able to walk home, let alone keep the flock in order. But Dickie gave him time to recover. He cooled his head, arms, and feet in the burn and finished off the food he had not been able to eat at midday.

Then, as soon as they began to make for home, he found to his delight that all the stubbornness, the panic, stupidity, and bewilderment had gone out of the flock. The ordeal that they had had to face was over. Perhaps too the dip had begun to work, and the ticks that had bothered them for weeks were no longer biting and itching. The smell of home was in their nostrils. They plodded steadily and obediently over the fell, stopping to nibble at the new heather shoots, baaing contentedly. Even the dog seemed to know that its stiffer duties were over. It trotted easily by the side of the shepherd, taking little runs now and then to right and left to keep up a show of vigilance. The evening was filled with the calling of plovers and curlews, and the western clouds were soft and tender. Andrew forgot the blunders of the morning and the fatigue of the afternoon, and felt only the contentment of the flock as they moved steadily homeward.

'Well, Andy,' said old Mr Ingram as they stood watching the sheep disperse over their hill. 'How did ye get on, then, with your first dipping?'

'He did fine, da,' said Dickie. 'But he'll feel it tomorrow. What are your arms like?'

'A bit sore.'

'Let me feel them. Aye, they're not bad. But ye'll have to have a bit more muscle there if ye're going to be a wrestler.'

'Who told you that I wanted to be a wrestler?'

'Oh, I got to know.'

'Aye, it's tough work handling them big old ewes. Did ye manage them all right, Andy?'

'He never flinched. There's plenty strength. A bit more muscle and he'll be ready to take on anybody.'

Before he got into bed Andy stripped off his shirt and looked at his arms. It was true that they were thin and that the muscle did not stand out as he wished it would. He wondered if there was any way of getting good biceps. Perhaps now that Dickie knew he wanted to be a wrestler he would show him a way.

13

An Unexpected Sparring Partner

Just beyond the outskirts of the village there lived an old man whom nobody had much to do with. He never came into the village, and spent most of his time looking after his goats. He spent so much time on them that those who knew him said that he had grown to look like a goat himself. Andrew had never seen the old man, but he often passed the little field where the nannies were kept, and had often stopped to look at the billy-goat tethered to a big stake on the open ground farther up the hill. It was a big, well-built animal, in some ways resembling the wild cattle, because it had a white coat and reddish ears that twitched backwards and forwards with a quick flicking movement. But it was not remote and aloof like the cattle. It always looked at Andrew as if inviting, or daring, him to come closer.

The goat fascinated him. In spite of the queer smell that came from it he could not help going up to it. At first he kept out of reach, because as soon as he came close it lowered its horns and came for him. He heard the chain rattle and saw it lift out of the rough grass and then go taut. When he saw that the chain held, he put out a hand and tried to get a grip on one of the horns. The goat ducked away from him and then struck upwards at him, but in spite of this rough gesture Andrew felt that if he was patient the goat would not be so vicious. He pulled a handful of leaves from a rowan that grew out of the goat's reach and held them out, and while the goat was pulling the food into its mouth he got hold of the horns with both hands. The goat gave an angry toss and he lost his grip, but he gave it more leaves and took another hold. It bucked again, but he held on and wrestled with it till his wrists began to ache.

He had not held on to the horns for long but he had enjoyed the tussle, and had the feeling that if he did not strain too hard and practised often enough he could master the billy. He waited for a few minutes, then gave it more rowan leaves and wrestled with it till he was tired.

He did not tell anyone where he had been and what he had been doing, but when he got home his aunt put down her knitting and began to sniff. 'There's a queer smell in here,' she said. 'Did you bring it in, Andrew? Where on earth have you been to bring a smell like that into the house?'

'Nowhere,' he replied.

'I could have sworn you brought it in. Mebbe the wind has changed a bit.'

Andrew went out into the yard, took off his jacket and washed his hands and face in the burn. He did not want anyone to know what he had been doing, because he was afraid of being laughed at. Fortunately his aunt made no more mention of the smell, and his uncle did not notice anything unusual.

From then on he could not keep away from the billy. The next time he went to see it he took a carrot from his uncle's garden. He was afraid that after its first experience it might distrust him, but it did not hesitate to take the carrot, and while it was munching it he got hold of it again by the horns. His palms were a bit sore from the first tussle, but he held on, and the goat responded almost playfully, as if it enjoyed the sport as much as the bribe. Minute by minute they tugged and wrestled, both enjoying the trial of strength. Once he got the goat down on to its knees, but it forced him up. He did not try to throw it again. Once was enough to begin with. He let it go and gave it more leaves. As he left he heard it bleating after him as if it did not want him to go.

From then onwards he tried not to let a day go without visiting the goat, winning it over first of all with a carrot or a crust or some greenery, then wrestling with it. It became a recognized ritual, boy and animal pitting their strength against each other; and with every encounter Andrew felt himself growing not only stronger but also more skilful and cunning. After a few days he had learnt how to catch the goat off balance, to seem to give way to it and then by a sudden pressure force it down, even to throw it as cowboys were supposed to throw steers. This was the practice that he needed and that none of the boys would give him. In a strange way, the goat became a real friend to him, as Cappy had become that lonely Saturday long ago.

Day by day he felt himself growing stronger and tougher. His grip was harder, and he could feel the muscles filling out and tightening the sleeves of his jacket. One night when he had stripped to the waist and was washing in the kitchen, his uncle said, 'There must be something that's agreeing wi' you, lad. Look at his muscles, Florrie. He's got arms on him like a prize-fighter.'

'It must be all the good food that he's getting,' said his aunt.

But Andrew knew that it was more than the food. It was his daily exercise that was hardening him, his secret practice with the sparring partner whom he told nobody about; and one day, looking at Billy's fat and flabby body, he knew that the time was not far off when he would be ready to take on his enemy and finally settle scores with him.

A few days later the boys were kicking a bladder around in the schoolyard. They did not have a ball to play with, but whenever a pig was killed in the village someone brought the bladder to school. It was kicked towards Andrew, and though he was not in the game he moved forward to boot it. But at that moment Billy ran between him and the bladder and they collided. Billy made as if to push Andrew away, but Andrew, for the first time, got under his guard and gripped him round the middle. He held him for only a few seconds before he let go, but in that short time he realized how flabby Billy was.

'He's not strong at all,' he thought to himself. 'He's as soft as a girl. If I can manage the goat, I'll manage him.'

They did not fight, but in that momentary encounter Andrew knew that he was now the stronger. All that he needed now was the challenge and opportunity to show that Billy's reign as the king of the school was coming to an end.

✑14✑

Learning to Wrestle

The weather after Whitsuntide was dry and sunny, and it was a torment to Andrew to have to spend so much time in school; but once lessons were over he was out and about playing down by the burn, watching the salmon come up to spawn, bird-nesting with Alec in the woods that grew round the edge of the estate, and walking the hill with the shepherd. Now that the shearing and dipping were over, Dickie had more time to spare, but he still kept a close watch on the flock. The lambs were now strong enough to look after themselves, but sometimes they would fall into one of the deep draining ditches and be unable to get out. So Dickie walked the hill regularly and often took Andrew with him.

Andrew had not yet broached the subject of wrestling, but one day when they were sitting on the side of the hill watching the flock grazing quietly around them, he said to the shepherd, 'Do you remember what you said about my muscles when we came back from the dipping?'

'I remember.'

Dickie was not very talkative, but there was not much that he forgot.

'Feel them now, then.'

'Dod, something has made a big improvement there, Andy. What have you been doing to get them as hard as that?'

'I've been wrestling.'

'So you've started, then. You must have found a good sparring partner somewhere. Who is it?'

'It's a goat.'

'What?'

'Mr Nattrass's billy.'

'What? I've heard some funny things in my time, but blow if I've heard of anybody practising with a goat.'

'Do you think it's made a difference?'

'I should think it has. Here, try a grip on me . . . Steady up, lad, you'll break my spine.'

'You said that if I had stronger muscles I could be a wrestler. Do you think I'm ready now?'

'You're a persistent young beggar, aren't you? What do you want me to do now?'

'Will you give me a few lessons?'

'Now?'

'If you can.'

'Well, there's nae time like the present. If you've taken the trouble to toughen yourself up, it's as much as I can do to give ye a bit of practice. Come on, jackets off and boots off, and we'll start.'

So Andrew began on the second stage of his preparation to be a wrestler. Dickie taught him how to interlock his hands to get a good grip, how to balance himself properly, then how to read what his opponent was going to do, to watch his feet, to learn from the pressures on his body what tricks were to be tried out on him, to know when to take the initiative, and when to lull his adversary into a false sense of security and throw him quickly and expertly. It was not an easy science to learn, and Andrew was very clumsy at first. All his colliery training was contrary to this kind of tussling. But Dickie was a patient teacher and Andrew was a good learner. He was quick on the uptake, and he was keen to excel. It was a queer thing to be doing there on the lonely hillside, wrestling with a man who was a champion. At first the dogs were a nuisance, but they soon learnt that it was nothing but a game; and the sheep grazed on, utterly indifferent to the rehearsals. Andrew no longer went to try his strength out on the goat, although every time he went past it bleated as if it could not understand why he had forsaken it. But he had more serious and earnest exercises now to go through; and when they were over and Dickie was confident that he had learnt the elements of the sport, Andrew took to going to see the shepherd wrestling at the local shows. Every village had its show and every show had its wrestling competition. Whenever Dickie entered, Andrew tried to see him compete, and when the sports were over he would go over the course of the bouts with him. Soon he had forgotten completely his old style of fighting and longed to try his hand at the new sport.

Now he did not shirk practice in the playground. His first bout was with Alec, who was no match for him. Then, just for fun, he began to take on some of the other boys. Now that he was one of them they were ready to have a go with him. At first he had a few disappointments. Practising with Dickie had not been a wholly satisfactory substitute for trying his skill against boys of his own age; but little by little he grew more confident, and more able; and the more victorious he grew the friendlier became the boys who for so long had so stubbornly declined to accept him.

There was only one boy whom he did not yet take on. It was Billy. When he defeated him, he meant it to be a spectacular defeat, not private but public. Dickie, who kept an eye on his progress, told him what to do. He advised him to put his name down for the schoolboys' wrestling contest at Lilburn Show. Billy had been the champion for years. If Andrew meant to get the better of him, this was his great opportunity.

∾15∾

Lord George Refuses to Help

A few days later Mr Dennison came back to Lilburn. 'Well, Mr Dennison,' said Mr Charlton, 'it's as good as a big apple to see you back in these parts. Have ye finished your pictures yet?'

'Yes, all done and ready to be presented to his lordship. I want you to bring Andrew up and have a look at them before I hand them over. But not just yet. I have some other news for you. I've been to see your mother, Andrew – and your father. You were right, boy – it was the Infirmary.'

'And how are they getting on at Sleetburn – at home?'

'Well, well – yes, things could be worse. Your brother is a good son, Andrew. He's making good money, and with that and the compensation your mother can make ends meet. She didn't complain, but . . .'

'What about my father?'

'There the news is not so good. He had a bad accident. You know that, don't you?'

'Yes.'

'I had a long talk with him, and I'm satisfied that in time he'll be as good as ever he was. But he's still in the Infirmary. There are come complications.'

'If they're serious ye'd better let us know, Mr Dennison. I want the lad to know just what the situation is.'

'Then I'll tell you what the doctor said.'

'Ye had a word with him?'

'Yes. He's a good doctor. But he doesn't think your brother-in-law will be out of bed much before Christmas.'

'That's a lang time for anyone to lie in bed.'

'Yes, but he won't let him up till he's certain that his legs are properly mended. So, Andrew, you'll have to stay with your uncle here, if he'll have you.'

'We'll have him, Mr Dennison. Nae two ways about that. To tell the truth, I think his aunt will brek her hairt when he has to leave us.'

'Then my advice to you, Andrew, is – be thankful for your uncle's offer. Your mother has a big family. I'm not saying you wouldn't be a help to her if you were at home. But the less she has to feed and look after the better . . . There now, that's settled. Now come up to the castle, both of you, and look at my pictures. You won't get much of a chance to see them once they've been handed over to Lord George.'

'I'd be grateful to come,' said Mr Charlton. 'I want to have a word with Hetherington and I can kill two birds wi' the one stone.'

Mr Dennison had worked hard while he had been away, and he had four big canvases to show them, magnificent views of the castle from different viewpoints. He had done these to satisfy Lord George, but he had done others to please himself, mainly sketches of the park and the cattle.

'I don't expect his lordship to be interested in these,' he said, 'but in years to come people may think more of my pictures of the herd than of the castle. I've got an idea the cattle will last longer than any bricks and stones.'

'They will if I have anything to do wi' it,' said Mr Charlton. 'That's what I've come to see the laird about. Just wait outside on the forecourt for me, Andrew. I'm hoping that I winna be long, but ye nivver ken.'

He had not been waiting long before he heard Lord George

and his uncle approaching. He knew that something had gone wrong with the interview, because the laird was speaking loudly and angrily.

'Hay?' he shouted. 'Since when have you started feeding the herd with hay?'

'I found out last year that when they're hard up for natural feed they'll tek a bit of hay or chopped straw. And it's a good job I did or else we would have lost mair than we did in the bad weather.'

'I thought they could look after themselves. Damn it, they're wild cattle, aren't they?'

'Even wild cattle can suffer in bad weather, and ye should be the first to knaw it.'

'Well, you're not getting any hay from me for them! If I have any to spare I'll sell it. Not waste it on beasts that don't need it.'

'Then ye winna give me onny?'

'Certainly not. Your father didn't molly-coddle the cattle and I'm not going to let you start.'

'I'm warning you, Hetherington. Lilburn has always had its herd of wild cattle. Your father used to boast about them and he had reason to. There's not another herd like this in the whole world. But if you go on like this the day will come when there winna be a single beast left.'

'That won't break my heart. I'll be glad to get rid of the expense. And I won't have to put up with your insolent ways either. Have you anything else to say?'

'Plenty, Hetherington. In my opinion ye ought to be ashamed of yersel. For seven hundred years the Hetheringtons have been here and the herd has been in their keeping. Ye may be prepared to see the end on't, but I'm not. It's my job to keep it alive.'

'Then do your job and don't come whining to me. You're getting above yourself, Charlton. It wasn't my father's practice to feed good hay to the herd, and it's not going to be mine. What's this boy doing here?'

'I dinna bring him. He came at Mr Dennison's invitation.'

'Then get him out of here. And let me tell you, I don't care for your way of speaking to me.'

'I speak my mind, Hetherington. Ye knew that when ye took me on.'

'You'd better mend your ways. If you don't show me more respect, you can pack up and find another job. I don't want a menial to tell me how to manage my estate. What do you say to that?'

'I say this. I've done my duty to you, Hetherington. Ye can get rid of me if ye like, but ye winna find another warden that will look after the herd the way I've done.'

'Yes, you have a good opinion of yourself.'

'I say what I have to say to your face, not behind your back.'

'And one of these days you'll say it too often. You're getting no hay from me, and if you don't like it, you can lump it. And don't bring that boy into my grounds again – or I'll send you both packing.'

With that he turned angrily away and went indoors.

'What are you going to do now, Uncle?' asked Andrew as they walked home.

'About the hay?'

'Yes.'

'If Hetherington winna give it to me, I'll just have to take it.'

'Without telling him?'

'Aye.'

'What if he finds out and gives you notice?'

'Nae fear of that. He's as daft as a brush but he kens a good servant when he sees yin. He'll make his tongue go – aye, he's good at that – but he winna get rid of me.'

85

'Why do you keep on here if you canna get on with him?'

'I dinna stop for his sake, hinny. It's the herd that keeps me here. It's my job in life to look after the cattle – and I'll stick to it for the rest of my puff. But we have a bit of gay dirty work in front of us, Andrew.'

'What are you thinking of?'

'Some way or other we've got to lay our hands on a bit of hay. And we have to find somewhere to keep it safe till the winter. We'll have to put our thinking caps on. They'll be starting on the intakes any day now.'

The second of the problems, where to keep the stolen hay, was unexpectedly solved by Alec. In spite of his smallness and slightness he was in some ways a more daring boy than Andrew, and less afraid of trespassing. Andrew had been so rudely treated by Lord George that he was scared of giving further offence, but Alec did not care what he did and where he went; and one day he took Andrew to see a cave that he had discovered in the castle grounds.

On the far side of the estate, between the castle and the park, there was an outcrop of grey rock. It was almost overgrown with heather and broom and ash trees, the roots of which ran like veins over the stones before burying themselves in the crevices and fissures. It seemed solid, but behind a ragged growth of thorns and furze Alec had found an opening. It had been boarded up some time ago, but the upper planks had been removed, and it was possible to climb over those that were left and get into the cave. When Andrew got over this barrier he saw that it was not an ordinary cave he had entered, for ten feet or so inside, the ground fell away dangerously, revealing a deep pit. The walls had been hewn out of the solid rock, and the pit, though covered at the bottom with brushwood, was as dry as a bone.

'This is just . . .' he said incautiously, but stopped himself in time.

'What did ye say?' asked Alec.

'It's just the place for a hidey-hole,' he said. 'Ye could camp out in here.'

He said no more, but when they had finished exploring, he told his uncle what he had found.

'Dod, it's just the verra place,' said Mr Charlton. 'That's one place I nivver thought about. By sangs, ye've only been here a few months, Andy, but ye ken mair about the place than some folks that have lived here all their lives. You're sure it's dry?'

'As dry as an oven.'

'It's a tidy walk from there to the intake, and we'll have to make sure the hay disna get foisty once it's in there. But that's the place, lad, and all credit to the pair of ye for finding it.'

Stealing Hay

It was getting on towards the end of July and close to Lammas when the men began to cut the hay. They were expecting a good crop from the two meadows, the Big Intake and the Little Intake, and the bailiff said he wanted as many men as possible in the fields. The Park Warden was not usually expected to help with this work, but Mr Charlton said he'd give a hand, partly because he wanted to keep on the right side of the bailiff, and partly because he wanted to keep an eye on the way the work was going.

It was a heavy crop and the weather was perfect for hay-making. Both the bailiff and Mr Charlton were pleased, the bailiff because he knew that he more he got in the better Lord George would like it, and the Warden because he knew that the bigger the crop the easier it would be for him to take his cut. The men moved in with their scythes, cutting spaces big enough to get the reaper in, and opening up the edges. Then the reaper was brought in, and all day long it went round and round the intake, whirling and clacking like a great grass-hopper. The men left the rows for a day or two, then turned them and tossed them, making sure the hay was perfectly dry before they piked it. Mr Charlton kept a close eye on the work. He knew that he had to choose the right moment for taking the hay – after it had dried out, but before it was piked.

The night before the men began to pike the Big Intake, Mr Charlton told Andrew to get ready. As soon as it was dark he lit two lamps in the cottage, let them burn for a few minutes, then put them out. Then they slipped outside and he locked the door. The evening was very still and filled with the smell of the stocks that grew outside the kitchen door. Not a light showed in any of the cottages. The men had had a hard day in the fields and had another hard one in front of them. The village was as silent as a tomb. Mr Charlton had hidden two hay-forks in the bracken on the far side of the intake. They took them out and forked up a bit of hay here and a bit there till they had a little pike ready to carry off to the cave.

Each with his forkful of hay, the shaft of the fork sloped over his shoulder, and the hay falling over his head and shoulders like a grotesque cowl, the man and the boy went backwards and forwards from meadow to pit, pit to meadow, never speaking or stopping, and seeing nothing but the dark path before them. Anyone coming upon them in the darkness might have fled from them as from two fearsome creatures of the night with vast supernatural heads. But no one saw them, and no one hindered their innocent pilfering. Their only witnesses were the sheep that coughed in the heather, and the cows that lay bedded down in the bracken.

Although it was late when they got to bed they were both in the field early to see if their theft had been noticed; but they had done their job well, and no one suspected that anything unusual had happened. The men set to work to pike the intake.

It was now the turn of the Little Intake. Mr Charlton and Andrew repeated the operation of the previous night. By midnight they had taken as much from both the meadows as they dared take.

'It's all a bit of a risk,' said Mr Charlton. 'If the hay turns foisty we'll have wasted some good fodder and our time as well. But there's a reasonable chance that it will keep, and if it does it will be worth its weight in gold.'

'What about boarding up the entrance?'

'I daren't start hammering at this time of the night.'

'Have you got any big screws?'

'I think I can lay my hands on one or two.'

'I'll come back tomorrow and screw the boards over the entrance.'

'And I'll sweetheart the bailiff to see if he'll let me have a spare pike for the herd. I heard him say it's the best hay-harvest he's had for years, and he's been grateful for what we've done. With a couple of pikes and what we've got there we should be reasonably ready for the bad weather.'

'Will they eat anything else?'

'They'll take a bit of oat-straw as weel.'

'Can you get any?'

'Nae trouble about that. Ye canna get any money for oat-straw so Hetherington will let me have a bit of that.'

After two nights Andrew was beginning to feel tired, but he got up and went to the field again early the next morning. All was well there. No one had noticed what they had taken. When they had finished piking Andrew went back home, found the screws that his uncle had ready for him, greased them, and took them to the cave. He covered the hay with brushwood, screwed the boards back into position, and concealed the path to the entrance with broken branches and bracken. When he got back to the field he found that his uncle had persuaded the bailiff to let him have a couple of pikes of the hay, and had even promised to cart it for him up to the park. Mr Charlton built a floor over the rafters in the shelter and they stored the hay there out of sight of the cattle and out of reach of the laird.

'There now,' said Mr Charlton. 'I feel easier in my mind than I've done for months. If only I'd had a bit more hay last year I would have saved them two calves we lost. Providing it's not ower bad a winter, we'll be able to keep the cattle in reasonable condition till the New Year comes in.'

∽17∽

Andy the Champion

The Schoolboys' Wrestling Championship was not the most important item on the programme for Lilburn Show, and since it was one of the events the organizers liked to have cleared out of the way before the serious business of the day was to begin – the men's wrestling, the piping and the sheepdog trials – the semi-finals were arranged for eleven in the morning and the finals at midday.

Dickie had told Andrew that one of the things he should do before the semi-finals was to take a good look at the field where they were to be held, test the grass in his stockinged feet, and look out for any holes or mounds that might make him stumble. As soon as the dew had dried he went to make his inspection, then for half an hour before the first bout he jogged up and down in a little copse just outside the field. Dickie had told him never to go into a contest without warming himself up, flexing the muscles of his arms and back and legs and making himself supple. It was a coldish day and he was glad of the exercise.

The semi-finals were soon over. His opponent was no match for him and was easily beaten. The other semi-final was over even more quickly. Alec, who had surprised every-body, including himself, by getting as far as this, knew that he was no match for the champion, Billy, and put up only a half-hearted show against him. When the bouts were over, Andrew put on his jacket and began to walk around the showground to keep warm. As he did his circuit he caught sight of Billy. He was sitting on the grass with his legs wide apart, eating a pie.

He looked strong and confident, but at the sight of him doing what Dickie had warned him never to do, Andrew felt his spirits rise.

But when the castle clock struck twelve and he went back to the field he was disconcerted to see that the man chosen to referee the final was Mr Ridley. He did not know that it was customary for the schoolmaster to supervise the final round. This was something that no one had told him. For a moment his confidence left him. For him Mr Ridley was the worst possible choice. As far as Andrew was aware he had never shown any interest in the sport and was even ignorant of the rules; and he had never forgotten how Andrew had set about him in the classroom and disgraced him with Mr Dennison.

None of the boys – or the men either for that matter – wore any special wrestling costume. Andrew and Billy simply stripped off their jackets, unlaced and took off their boots, and prepared for the bout. There were not many spectators, but as Mr Ridley called them up, Andrew saw Dickie take his place beside his uncle, and he knew that he had at least two well-wishers in the crowd.

He took a deep breath and the exciting smell of the crushed grass rose in his nostrils. It was a smell that somehow thrilled and heartened him. He felt strong, relaxed, and unafraid.

'First bout!' called Mr Ridley, and Andrew leant forward to take his grip, but his fingers had barely touched when he felt himself being seized. He gave way to the strain as Dickie had taught him, his hands groping for the hold they had not been allowed to find, but Billy arched away from him, held him off, and suddenly kicked his legs away. Andrew managed to keep his balance, although he was hurt by the kick, but there was nothing for him to hold on to. Billy hooked his leg round him a second time. He lost his balance and fell and the bout was given against him.

He jumped up, burning with fury at the trick that had been played on him, and at Mr Ridley's unfairness in not seeing that he had been fouled. He knew now what to expect. Billy was out to win by fair means or foul, and Mr Ridley was there to favour him. He knew too that his opponent would not be able to use the same trick twice. When Mr Ridley called 'Second bout!' he was on his guard. He leant forward, shuffling his body and arching it, not allowing Billy to take grip until he had found his own and locked his fingers securely together.

He could feel that Billy was a little taken aback. Perhaps he had counted on playing the same unfair trick again, and had not reckoned on Andrew's seeing so quickly through his game. Andrew knew in the first seconds of the bout that he had thrown his opponent out of his stride, but he resisted the temptation to throw him there and then, and gripped him harder and harder till he could hear Billy begin to pant and grunt. Andrew knew that the longer the contest lasted the better it would be for him. He tightened his hold around Billy's flabby middle till he could feel him beginning to tire. Then, at the right moment, he feinted with his right leg, felt Billy alter his stance to counter the attack and go off balance. He closed quickly, got his hip under him, threw him, and pinned his shoulders to the ground. The scores were now even.

Mr Ridley looked as disconcerted as his favourite. He took a long time before calling them together again, to give Billy time to get his wind back. At last the bout was announced, and Billy wiped his nose in an ugly way on his thumb and forefinger and came up ponderously for the last decisive clinch. He was red and puffed. Andrew could see that the long second bout had taken it out of him. He looked vexed and vicious. Andrew knew that he would have to be more careful than ever.

They leaned forward and took grip. Again Andrew was careful not to be caught napping, but while they crouched, locked together, rocking slightly from one leg to another and revolving slowly now to the left, now to the right, Billy suddenly jerked his head upwards and sideways. His hard skull caught Andrew on the temple and for a moment knocked him dizzy. He felt Billy's leg lift and strike again against his sore calf, and he almost went over; but somehow he kept his balance, the dizziness passed, and in its place came an angry determination to put an end once and for all to the contest and to the underhand tricks that Billy was playing.

'You pig, Billy Craggs,' he said and pulled so hard that he heard him gasp with the violence of his grip. Andrew suddenly felt that, if he wanted to, he could break Billy's back-bone like a clay pipe. He pulled him to him, let him go, pulled him in again, and set him shuffling now this way, now that. Billy began to breathe heavily, as he used to do in the playground when he had had enough of a game, and Andrew knew that he had mastered him just as he had learnt to master that obstinate old goat on which he had practised. He manœuvred him skilfully till he had him just where he wanted him. He gave a sharp pull, felt the fat and hateful body yielding, hooked his right leg under it, and sent it sprawling. There was no need for him to leap upon it and pin the shoulders down. Billy was finished and the match was over. It was only when the cheering had stopped and Dickie was with him clapping him on the shoulder that he felt his cheek wet, and realized that the wetness was not sweat but blood.

For the rest of the afternoon he walked around the ground in a daze, hardly knowing what he was looking at or what was being said to him. Even the men's wrestling seemed to be taking place at a distance from him, and when he was told Dickie had won again, he hardly took it in.

He behaved so strangely that old Mr Ingram took him into the tea-tent to let the bone-setter have a look at him.

'I think the lad's got a touch of concussion,' said the bone-setter. 'He must have had a terrible crack on his skull to daze him like this.'

'It was that beggar, Billy Craggs,' said Mr Ingram. 'Dod, he should be drummed out of the village for playing a trick like that. And as for that Ridley – that's the last time he'll ivver umpire a final if I have anything to do with it.'

But Andrew did not mind. He felt shaken and muzzy, but when he heard his uncle say, 'Weel done, Andy! That Billy Craggs has been king bull in Lilburn fair ower lang. It's time he was taking a back seat. Just wait till Mr Dennison hears that ye're the champion. He'll be gay proud – but not half as proud as I am to see my own nephew cock of the walk in Lilburn' – then he felt that he had come to the happiest day in all his life.

∽18∾

A Sharp Frost

At last all the shows were over, the holiday at an end, and the long northern winter began. At first Andrew did not like the long, dark evenings. He still missed the games in the street, the noisy running up and down the colliery rows, the fighting and squabbling under the street lamps. The boys of Lilburn did not play in the dark as they did at Sleetburn. They preferred to stay indoors, to stay by the warm peat fires, to go to bed early.

But Andrew soon found there was plenty to do. He went as often as he could to see the shepherd and old Mr and Mrs Ingram, to listen to the old man playing his pipes and to hear the old woman singing. She knew a lot of songs, some of them very funny ones about Tyneside, about someone who missed the train, and about a famous pawnshop that had burnt down. She could sing other songs about Hobbie Noble, Flodden Field, and the Death of Parcy Reed, but the ones he liked best were 'Cushie Butterfield' and 'The Lambton Worm'. Dickie did not play the pipes or sing, but he taught Andrew how to carve the horn of a blackface ram into the shape of a trout or a fishing heron. He was a good carver and won prizes for his carvings which he made into an ornamental crook.

It was quieter at home, but his aunt and uncle were very fond of cards and dominoes, and they spent many happy hours playing rummy and three-handed whist and crib.

Mr Dennison had gone for good, but from time to time he wrote to Mr Charlton asking him about the herd, and Mr Barnes wrote to Andrew, telling him how his father was back at home and beginning to get onto his feet. Sleetburn seemed a long way away now. In spite of himself Andrew had grown fond of his new way of life, and did not want to change it.

Autumn merged quickly into winter. Christmas, mild and wet and green, came and went and New Year's Day came on its heels. Everyone went first-footing, and after Mr Charlton had let in their first foot, he and Andrew went off to be first foot to old Mrs Ingram.

It was long after one o'clock when they left the shepherd's cottage, but they did not go home. They went off to the park.

'I always like to tek a look at the herd the first thing I do in the New Year,' said Mr Charlton. 'Just to bring them luck.'

The night air was cold and sharp. The land was flooded with the weak light of the moon. It was waning and looked odd and lopsided. It was hanging high in the dark sky, shining with a sad and diminished power; but all around it the stars were brilliant, jagged, and sharp as spurs. The lights were still on in all the farms and cottages. All the folk like good Northumbrians were keeping the New Year. But as Andrew and his uncle went up the hill they saw the lamps go out, and the park lay before them, silent and vast and dark. Below them they could see the milky forms of the cattle bedded down on the dark earth, and in the distance the looming shape of the fell. The air was still and cold, and they could feel the frost tightening around everything.

'They look settled enough,' said Mr Charlton. 'You would think they knew it was the New Year, wouldn't you? Come on, Andy, time for us to get bedded down as well.'

They went to bed, but towards morning Andrew was wakened by the kind of noise he had heard on his second night in Lilburn. The bulls were fighting again. One more rival had decided to do his best to dethrone the king bull.

Night after night they kept up the bellowing, until it suddenly ceased. Suddenly in the middle of the night an extraordinary silence descended on the countryside, as if, in a second, the whole herd, bulls, heifers, and calves had been spirited away. More perturbed by the silence than by the noise of the fighting, Mr Charlton could not rest until he had found out what had happened. As soon as it was light he went to the park. An hour later Andrew saw him running back to the cottage.

'What's happened, Uncle?'

'By gox, tha'll nivver believe it, Andy. I've nivver seen onnything like this – nivver.'

'Has there been a fight?'

'Aye, that there has. The young bull's finished.'

'Did the king kill it?'

'Aye, but he did something else.'

'What?'

'He killed hissel.'

'How did he do that?'

'Oh, I can see what happened. He went for the young 'un, and got him, just here, under the hairt. He must have stopped his hairt just like stopping a clock. But he brok his own neck in the process. So they're both there, as dead as mutton, the pair of them.'

'Which one will be the king bull now?'

'One of the young 'uns. They'll all gan off somewhere and fight it out. I only hope to God they dinna kill ower many afore they settle it. But what a way to start the winter – nowt but a young bull to be the king! Pray to God we get good weather from now on, bonny lad. If we dinna, it's God help the poor beasts. I was hoping the old bull wad see the winter out, 'cos although he looked a scruffy devil he was a good bull and he gave us some good calves.'

'How many are there in the herd now?'

'We're down to twenty-eight now. I wanted to start the winter wi' thirty. If the weather behaves itsel' we'll be safe, but if we get a bad spell we could be in trouble. Keep thy fingers crossed, lad. We'll need all the luck we can get.'

Later in the day they went out to recover the carcases of the dead bulls. Once more the groom was sent into the park on horseback with some of the hounds to keep the herd away till the bodies were loaded on to the carts and taken to the butchers. This time joints were sent round to all the tenants and workmen as a New Year's gift, but as usual Cappy got everything that came to the Charltons.

'It seems an awfu' waste to give good meat like this to a dog,' said Mrs Charlton, 'but your uncle would choke if I put it on the table for him.'

All that night Mr Charlton was so troubled that he could not bring himself to take part in the nightly game of cards or dominoes, and the sight of him sitting dumbly before the fire reminded Andrew of that other occasion when the first bull had been found drowned. His uncle's misery made him uneasy and he went out so as to be out of the way for a while. He took Cappy with him. The dog was now used to him, and could be relied on not to run away.

As he went out he felt the ice in the ruts in the roadway cracking under his feet, and when he came back into the garden he put his hand into the trough under the pump. A thin layer of ice had formed on the surface. He tried the pump and noticed that the drops that splashed on the flagstones turned to ice as soon as they met the stone. The sky overhead was hard and black like the shell of a beetle. The frost was whitening the rough tufts of grass in the field beyond the garden. It was going to be a hard frost.

∾19∾

The Rescue

This was the beginning of a long frost. The ice that had formed over the water in the pump trough thickened day by day until it was solid. Big daggers of ice grew outwards from the banks of the burn, first over the pools where the water ran slowly, then over the quicker reaches. Then they met, and after a few days you could walk from bank to bank and never hear a crack. There was not enough room to skate, but the boys made slides where the pools had been, throwing themselves from one bank, sliding across the ice and leaping up on to the opposite bank. In spite of the sacking and straw that Mr Charlton wrapped round the pump, it iced up, and from then on they had to rely on the spring for drinking water, and break the ice in the burn for washing water. Every day it grew harder and harder to find a place where the burn was not frozen solid.

The weather was fine and clear, but from time to time there were snow showers that lay on the grass like sugar on a cake. Against the snow the shadows of the bare trees were like veins, blue and branching. All the day long the air was cold and keen. Mr Ridley taught in his overcoat and never strayed far from the fire; in their cold desks the children shivered, dancing their feet up and down to keep the circulation going. Before Andrew went to bed his aunt built up the fire and gave him the warm oven-shelf wrapped in flannel to take to bed with him. It was so cold that the milk froze, and one day Mrs

Charlton found a pan of broth that she had left beside the window in the pantry frozen as solid as the water in the trough. Andrew was glad of the thick socks, gloves, and wristbands that he had knitted for himself in the evenings before Christmas.

Day by day the birds came nearer and nearer to the house, fighting savagely for the scraps that were thrown out to them. Many of them died during the night, and sometimes their stiff little bodies were found under the bushes. The laurel and privet leaves curled and shrivelled, and a row of wallflowers that Mr Charlton had put in under the kitchen window hung black and limp.

After about ten days of bitter cold the glass began to drop.

'Dod, we're in for some bad weather, Florrie,' said Mr Charlton, tapping the glass and fiddling with the pointer. 'I've nivver seen the glass drop like this, and there's been a terrible bruff around the moon the last two nights. We're in for a fall of snow, as sure as I'm here.'

A few hours later a strange leaden cloud began to swell and thicken over Cheviot. The sky went a strange colour like the colour of blaeberry juice. Then the snow that Mr Charlton had prophesied began to fall. The children were in school when it began. Through the window Andrew could see the first flakes descending with a vague hesitant movement. They were as big as pennies, but they drifted waveringly through the air, falling, rising again, sliding away out of sight as if reluctant to come to rest. When Mr Ridley opened the door to see how heavy the fall was likely to be, they seemed to make a rush at him as if they meant to force their way into the room. Then they began to fall faster and more seriously as if their playful mood had left them and they were settling to their earnest business of covering the earth. Faster and more rapidly they came down, until when Mr Ridley opened the door again the ground was a foot deep in snow. An hour later he announced that he was going to close the school. He said that he wanted to make sure that all the boys and girls who had come a long way would get home safely, but they all knew that he was concerned about himself and wanted to get back to his own cottage.

But as it turned out, Mr Ridley had taken a wise precaution. By night-time the snow was so deep that even the men found it difficult to force a way through it, and instead of slipping to the ground it was massing on the branches of the trees in a dangerous manner. Even before the end of the day strange noises were heard all over the village and the castle grounds. It was the sound of branches being torn from the trunks by the intolerable weight of the snow. Over and over again men were wakened during the night by the same rending sound, as if some furious giant had broken loose and was tearing the trees limb from limb.

The next morning there was ruin everywhere. Almost every large tree had lost a bough and their trunks were scarred with big gashes. Some of the smaller trees had been bent right over by the snow until they had broken. The churchyard wall was completely buried and the road up to the castle was impassable. Mr Charlton could not get the kitchen door open. He had to climb out through a window and clear the snow away first. Then he had to dig a way to the spring before he could get any water. There was no possibility of getting to school. Everyone took it for granted that Mr Ridley was as snow-bound as the rest of the village.

Happily it had stopped snowing. The snow was too deep for sledging but the boys made a huge snowman, then turned it into an effigy of Mr Ridley and pelted it.

It was out of the question to try to clear away the fallen timber. The broken branches lay like fallen stags, the black boughs rearing out of the snow like antlers. All work in the village was brought to a standstill and the men were set to work clearing the castle forecourt and drives, but there was little point to all their labour. The village was cut off from the outside world. As far as anyone knew the whole of Northumberland was buried under the snow.

For most of the people of Lilburn being snow-bound was not a new experience, and they had had the good sense to prepare for it. There were stores of potatoes buried under straw in the earths, flour in the bins, fruit in preserving jars, and eggs pickled in isinglass. Most of the cattle had been housed in the byres and the horses were stabled. The mare that the shepherd and the warden had between them had been brought down from the hill and lodged in a lean-to at the side of the Charltons' cottage. But Dickie was worried about his sheep. He had not been able to get all his flock down from the hill and was anxious about the older ewes that were in the habit of feeding on the higher slopes of the fell. Mr Charlton was even more concerned for his herd. He had not seen them since the first snow-fall. He had no idea where they were, and what was worse, he could do nothing to help them.

He settled down to wait as patiently as he could for a thaw. But no thaw came. Instead the glass dropped even lower, the snow began to fall again, and a strong wind began to blow in from the east, driving the snow through every crack in window and door, and piling it high in huge drifts. It heaped it in great frozen dunes, moulding it into beautiful but fearful shapes, curved and edged like ploughshares. All the paths and roadways that had been cleared were blocked once more, and the land around the village looked like an arctic plain, bleak and limitless.

But somehow paths had to be trodden through the snow. Tracks were made from house to house and even Dickie managed to get down from his father's cottage; but what he had to say about the drifts on the higher slopes of the fells made Mr Charlton more and more anxious to find out what was happening to the cattle in the park. He was afraid that if the snow lasted long enough they would starve, and the thought that there was hay and straw for them in the shelter if only he could get them to it tormented him.

One day after dinner he told his wife that he was going to make a bid to reach them, and that he was going to take Cappy with him.

'Mercy on us, man, you're not taking that dog, are ye? Ye ken what he's like. He'll frighten the wick out of the cattle if he gets anywhere near them.'

'That's just what I'm hoping for, Florrie. If he frightens them, they'll make a noise. And if they make a noise I'll have some idea where they are.'

'Take care of yersel, then.'

'I will.'

'And what about me, Uncle?' asked Andrew. 'Can I come?'

'Nay, ye'd better stop here and keep your aunt company. I'm ganna try to get up to the shelter, although I might venture a bit farther if the herd's not there and the snow's not ower deep. Dinna worry, now. I'll be back afore dark.'

Andrew watched him cross the road and begin to climb. At first Cappy raced around him as if the snow and the freedom had driven it crazy, burying its snout in the fall and flinging it about wildly, but once they had crossed the trodden part of the roadway it was forced to keep behind its master, following in the narrow track that the warden was making. Andrew watched them till they were out of sight, then went indoors and sat down to wait for their return.

An hour passed, then a second hour and a third; but neither dog nor man had returned. When the afternoon began to go, and the snow began to fall again, Mrs Charlton began to be anxious.

'Pray God nothing's happened to your uncle, Andrew,' she

said. 'I'm not ower concerned about him, but ye nivver ken what will happen in snow like this. I wish we had Dickie here.'

'Would you like me to go and see if he's coming? I can light the stable lantern and that might help him if he's lost.'

'Give him a few mair minutes, hinny. Then take the lantern as far as ye can and shine it up the lonnen.'

By now it was dark, although from time to time Andrew saw the clouds thinning and a brightness seemed to filter through them as if there was a moon somewhere. He took a new candle out of the cupboard, then, seeing a little bottle of brandy on the shelf, put that in his pocket as well. The lantern was kept in the stable, and when Andrew took it down and lit it, the mare looked round at him, then got to her feet as if to come with him. He had not thought of taking the mare, but it struck him that if anything had happened to his uncle, he might be glad of her, if only to carry him the last few hundred yards. He put a halter on her and drew her out of the stable. She drew back a bit when she felt the cold air, but shook her head and followed him obediently across the roadway.

Luckily the snow began to ease off and began to fall lightly, with big feathery flakes that drifted indolently downwards. Beyond the first bend the track ran in the lee of a clump of evergreens and the drifts were smaller there. So long as he was in the shelter of the evergreens the going was not hard, but once he got out of the shelter of the bushes he found himself in trouble. He began to sink up to his thighs in the snow, and at every step the mare had to lift her hooves so high that she began to hang back; and with the double effort of pulling her and lifting his own legs clear of the snow, Andrew began to sweat. He could feel his body beneath the layers of clothes getting hotter and hotter, as if the heat was building up in him as it did in a damp haystack. In spite of the cold air he undid the buttons of his coat and loosened his muffler. He had not realized how exhausting it would be wading through this deep clogging snow.

Fortunately, when he got to the top of the rise the clouds began to part, and their edges were vaguely fringed with the hidden moon. In the weak diffused light he could see the park, a vast white wilderness, with nothing visible above the undulating expanse of snow but the tops of trees and the roof of the shelter. He felt sure his uncle had come this way because there were tracks leading towards the shelter, blurred and partly filled with the new snow, but still discernible.

But it was impossible to take the mare any farther. He turned back and led her into the shelter of a clump of hollies, and tethered her there, tying the rope very carefully to a thick branch. He knew that before the night was over he would need her.

Then he turned back to try to follow his uncle's traces, but he found himself in very deep snow. He had to fight his way step by step now, hauling his leg at every pace clear of the snow. His progress was snail-like, and he had a strange feeling that the snow was in some way snaring and engulfing him. Seeing the shelter still a long way ahead, and the clump of hollies far behind him, he began to lose the desire to go on, and to feel a great temptation to struggle no more but sink in the snow and let it swallow him; but just when, almost overpowered by the bewildering heat of his body, he was about to give in and sink into the drift, he felt his foot come down on something solid. It was the park wall. He got both feet on it, and stood up, precariously but with great relief, high above the treacherous snow. This, he saw, was what his uncle had done. He could see the footmarks turn and follow the line of the wall. He went where they led, but it was like walking an invisible tightrope, and his boots kept slipping. He was just beginning to wonder how far he would have to go on like this when he heard Cappy. It was not barking, but whining in a peculiar way, breaking every now and then into a short yap, as if it wanted to say something unusual but did not know how to. In his excitement Andrew stumbled, lost hold of his lantern, saw it fall in the snow and the candle go out with a fizz. It was impossible to relight it. He had not thought to bring any matches with him. But at that moment the moon swam out of the clouds. It was in its last quarter and its light was feeble and exhausted, but it was enough to show him first Cappy, sitting on the top of the wall, and then his uncle, face downward and half buried in the snow.

He let himself carefully down into the drift and brushed the snow from his uncle's head. His face was as cold as ice, but he was still breathing. His body was warm, in spite of the fact that his coat had been pulled open so violently that some of the buttons had been ripped off, and the neck of his shirt was open. Andrew turned the body over as best he could, and then saw what had happened. His uncle had slipped on the wall and hit his head against it. There was a wound on the right temple, and the blood had frozen over it.

'Come here, Cappy,' he said to the dog. 'Come down, boy.'

The dog jumped down and he made it lie close to his uncle's head. Then he eased the body over a bit more till the neck and shoulder were resting against the warm body of the dog.

Then he took out the brandy and poured it into his uncle's mouth. It was difficult to keep from spilling it, and he was afraid that it would run away and be wasted, but to his relief his uncle began to move his head as if the liquid was stinging him. He opened his mouth and Andrew poured more brandy into it. He swallowed it and opened his eyes.

'Is that you, Andrew?' he asked.

'Yes, it's me, Uncle.'

'Is it time to get up, then?'

'You're not in bed.'

'Where am I, then?'

'You're in the park. You've fallen in a drift.'

'Nivver. Not me, lad. I nivver . . . what's happened to me, Andy? Did I give in?'

'No, Uncle. You've hurt your head. You . . . it must be concussion, like I had when Billy Craggs gave me that knock. It must have dazed you. But you'll have to get up, Uncle. We have to get back. Would you like another drop of brandy?'

'Just pour another drop in.'

This time Mr Charlton took a good swallow. It seemed to do him the world of good and he began to struggle to get up.

'Did you find the herd?' he asked.

'I never looked for it, Uncle Adam. I came to find you.'

'I thought I saw them, and then my feet gave way.'

'Don't worry about the herd, Uncle. You'll have to get up on to the wall again. Can you manage?'

'I'll try. But I feel queer, hinny. Lad, I've nivver felt as bad as this. But I'll try.'

It was a struggle to get him out of the drift and on to the wall. He went a few steps and then fell again. Andrew had never seen him like this. He did not seem to know where he was or where to move.

'It's nae good, Andy,' he said. 'I'll nivver manage it. Ye'd better get back and fetch somebody to help me.'

'There isn't time for that, Uncle. Get down on your hands and knees. Crawl if you cannot walk. It isn't far, and I've got the mare waiting for us.'

His uncle did not seem to understand what was being said to him, but bit by bit Andrew got him to crawl along the wall until they came to the point where they had to leave it. Then began the worst stretch of all. It was bad enough to get through the deep snow with no encumbrance. Now that he had to stop at almost every step and rouse his uncle to keep moving he began to be afraid that they would both collapse. He felt again the strong desire to give in, to sink down in the white depths of the snow and let it close over him. But he made his uncle take more brandy, and even swallowed some himself, though he hated the taste of it; and at last he saw the mare waiting patiently where he had left her.

His uncle had fallen again, and Andrew did not know how he would get him onto the mare's back, but he managed to rouse him once more, and got him in a sitting position on the top of another stretch of wall. Then he moved the mare over to him, and pushed him until he lay slumped across her back. The mare was wonderful. She seemed to know what was expected of her and stood still while Andrew manœuvred the heavy body till it was lying along her back. Then pulling off his muffler he ripped it from top to bottom. With one half he tied his uncle's hands under the mare's neck, and with the other his legs under her girth. Then he knew that the worst was over.

The mare was magnificent right up to the end of that nightmare journey. She moved downhill slowly and carefully. Usually she broke into a trot when she was nearing her stable, but this time she did not even quicken her pace. He walked her quietly almost up to the kitchen door. Within a few minutes neighbours had come and Mr Charlton was safe in his bed.

When Andrew took the mare back to her stable he took off the halter and stood with his arms around her neck. He did not want to go indoors. He was trembling from head to foot. He began to cry, wondering if the tears would ever stop and he would be able to go into the house without letting everybody know that he had been crying like a baby.

20

The Survivors

It took Mr Charlton a long time to recover from his accident. The concussion he had suffered was not serious, but shock and exposure brought on pneumonia, and for many days he was seriously ill. During the crisis of his illness he grew delirious, and rambled endlessly about his cattle. His deepest anxiety was that the herd would starve before they could get help, that the cattle he had given all his working life to care for would be lost for ever, and the priceless creatures that his forebears had kept alive for centuries perish through his ill fortune and neglect. Nor could Andrew have consoled him even if he had been well enough to listen to him, for the park was still buried deep in snow and no one knew if the cattle were alive or dead.

Then Andrew began to realize that although he had saved his uncle's life once, he would have to save him a second time by bringing him, somehow or other, reassuring news about the herd. At one time he thought of going on his own initiative to plead with Lord George and persuade him to send men up to the park to search for the cattle, but he felt the laird would never listen to him. It had never mattered to him whether they lived or died. Nor could Andrew ask Dickie to help. He was far too busy feeding his flock and making sure that as many as possible of those left on the hill were rescued. The more Andrew thought about it the more he realized that he would have to act on his own.

At first he had unexpected helpers. The school was still closed, and the boys had time to themselves. When Andrew began clearing the path up to the park, five or six of them brought shovels and helped him. After a day or two most of them found this too dull a way of passing the time, and in the end only Alec stayed by him; but with their help he had cleared a reasonably wide path up to the park wall.

Happily no more snow fell. The weather was cold but not stormy, and though there was a hard crust of ice over the snow it was soft underneath and not hard to shift. In two more days the boys had got through to the shelter, cleared a space under it, and pulled down some of the hay and straw that Mr Charlton had stored in the loft. After that they could do no more but wait to see if any of the cattle would find their way to the shelter.

It was a cold business waiting hour by hour by the wall, and Alec soon gave it up, but Andrew got a fire going by the wall and passed the time away, grilling pieces of bacon like a tramp, and roasting potatoes in the embers.

For two cold long days he kept his vigil. Then at last he saw what he was waiting for – the first survivor. It was a solitary bull. It came out of the wall of snow like a lonely explorer emerging from an arctic waste – thin, shambling, emaciated. But it was alive. It found the hay and began to eat it.

Then later in the day a second bull, and after it three heifers, appeared. They were pitifully weak, so thin that Andrew was glad his uncle was not there to see them. Their hip bones stood out from the lank flesh as if they were about to push their way through the thin hide, and they were so desperate for food that they fought among themselves for the hay that was laid out for them. Andrew had never heard of bulls and heifers fighting before, but now the survivors had only one desire – to eat and live on.

All that day Andrew stood by the wall watching the pitiable

creatures eating, butting one another away feebly, guarding whatever mouthful of fodder they had, mournful wrecks of the fine animals they had been before the coming of the dreadful snow. Only one more survivor appeared, but by the end of the day Andrew had learnt that at least six of the herd were still alive, and that although no calf seemed to have lived through the storm, four of the six still living were heifers.

Now it was time for him to draw on the supply of hay that his uncle and he had hidden in the cave. Another path had to be cleared, and this time he had no help. But Andrew was no longer the boy who had been upended so easily by Billy Craggs on his first day in Lilburn. Good food, months in the keen Northumbrian air, tough exercise, and hard work had made him hardy and muscular and full of stamina. He shifted the snow, cleared the mouth of the cave, and then, forkful by forkful, carried the hay down to the shelter. He had learnt how to work in the fashion of countryfolk, not hurrying, not overstraining himself, not driving himself madly to the end of his resources, but slowly and patiently, without exhausting himself. By now the cattle had learnt where to find the fodder, and Andrew had learnt their habits. When he was sure he was not disturbing them, he left the fodder for them, then kept well out of the way so that they could feed without being alarmed. And by now he had counted ten survivors, six of them heifers.

Nothing, said the doctor, helped Mr Charlton to recover as this news did. The thought that the herd had not after all utterly perished, and that there were bulls and heifers enough left for it to recover and multiply, was better for him than the medicines he could prescribe. From then onwards he lived only for the day when he could see with his own eyes the cattle that had been so wonderfully preserved.

And then, at last, the thaw came. One night when they

were all sitting before the fire, Mr Charlton suddenly looked up.

'Listen!'

Andrew thought that he heard a noise from the park, but the sound he had caught was the dripping of water from the thatch.

'It's the thaw,' he said. 'I can hear and I can feel it. Thanks be to God, the snow's melting at last. Slip out, Andrew, and see what's happening.'

Andrew went out. The air had grown warm, water was running from the roof, and already there was a thin film of moisture over the ice in the trough. The long frost was ending. After six weeks of continuous ice the world was melting, and the great blanket of snow dissolving and thinning and running into the softening earth.

∽21∽

Back to Sleetburn

From then on, as if the year had repented of its wicked behaviour, the skies cleared, the sun shone warmly, and a soft drying wind began to blow. The snow thinned, turned brown, and tarnished, then vanished like smoke. The grass emerged, green and new, and the horses, cows, and sheep went out again to eat their fill of the sweet spring herbage; and at last the time came when Mr Charlton was well enough to go up to the park and see for himself how his cattle were faring.

It was early March, but already the curlews were calling, and the plovers kept rising in wavering flight from the ground, their white bodies gleaming as their wings rose and fell. Big white clouds rose and swelled over the dark shapes of Cheviot and Hedgehope, and sailed across the sky like white petals blown across a pond. The resinous smell of pine and fir blew from the plantations.

His long illness had left Mr Charlton weak. He no longer went striding ahead as he had done on that first walk to the park almost a year ago. But he was impatient to see his beloved herd again. When he saw them all mustered near the shelter, as if they had known he was coming to inspect them, his eyes shone.

'There they are,' he said, 'and, thank God, they're not as weak and wambly as I thought they might be. But surely there's mair there than we expected, isn't there? Can it be possible that one or two mair have kept alive?'

Andrew counted them quickly. His uncle was right. From somewhere or other three more beasts had appeared. But they saw no more, either on that or any other day. Out of the thirty that had been alive before the storm, seventeen had died. Somewhere in the bracken and heather, perhaps still half hidden in the last of the drifts, lay the bones of seventeen victims, their flesh torn from them by hungry foxes and their bleached skeletons picked clean by crows and magpies.

'What do you think of them, Uncle?' asked Andrew. 'Do you think they're coming on?'

'They're not bad,' said Mr Charlton. Andrew could see that something was still troubling him.

'What's up, Uncle? Is there something the matter with them?'

'The bulls look good enough. That'll be the one that came out first, is it?'

'Yes.'

'He'll be the king bull most likely. Ay, he's a good-looking beast.'

'He's better looking than the old one we had.'

'He's a bit on the lean side, but he'll fatten. It's not him I'm worried about. It's the heifers.'

'Why?'

'We'll no get a calf from any of them this year.'

'Why not?'

'I ken these heifers as weel as if they were my ain bairns. There's nine of them, but not one of them will calve this year. Five of them's past it. They're fair ower old to calve.'

'And what about the others?'

'Ower young. There's not one of them that is much mair than three, and a wild heifer from this herd nivver comes into season afore she's four. Ye can see what that means, can't ye?'

'Yes.'

'We're stuck at thirteen – a gay unlucky number – and not

115

a hope of increasing it. If we get mair bad weather next winter it could be less. Still we must be thankful for what we have. We might all have snuffed it – cows and keeper and all.'

Mrs Charlton was waiting for them at the door when they got back.

'Have ye seen the herd?' she asked.

'Aye, I've seen them, Florrie, and my mind's at rest now. There's mair of them left than we thought, and they're all bonny as ivver they were.'

'Well, that's good news now,' said Mrs Charlton. 'And they're not the only ones that have come round. Look at this, Andrew.' And she held out a letter that had just come.

It was a letter from his father, the first he had been able to write to him. He was almost completely recovered now, and the doctor had told him that he could begin work again.

> I cannot tell you, Florrie, [he wrote] how much we are in your debt for taking Andrew off our hands for such a long time. It's well nigh a year now since he came to stop with you and we'll never forget your kindness in giving him a home. If all we hear is true he has enjoyed himself and made a bit of a mark in Lilburn. But we cannot expect you to keep him for ever and now that I'm back at work and addling a decent wage it is time he was coming home. If he tells us which day he is coming and when the train gets into Durham Jack will come for him with the trap.

'So we'll have to manage without ye, hinny,' said Mrs Charlton. 'We'll miss ye. Ye've been grand company.'

'Aye, and mair than good company,' said her husband. 'If it had not been for him dear kens where I would ha' been by now. But all good things must come to an end, Andy. We'll have to start packing his traps, Florrie.'

'I bet ye'll be excited. It's a lang time for a lad to be away from his own home.'

'Yes, I am excited, Aunt Florrie,' he said.

But he wasn't. Once he would not have been able to sleep at the prospect of going to Sleetburn and being able to stay out in the dark playing Tally-ho and Knocky-nine-door with the lads of the colliery. But now he did not want to go. He did not want to leave the village and the cattle and Alec and the shepherd and Mr and Mrs Ingram. Lilburn was his home now, and he wanted to stay there.

On Sunday he went to church for the last time. It was a fine day and the church was nearly full. During the service the parson gave thanks for the end of the winter and for the recovery of Mr Charlton; and he preached a sermon on the receding of the waters after the flood in the bible, and told how Noah's animals had at last been able to walk out into the dry fields and feed and grow fat.

When the service was over the congregation stayed behind, as they often did, to talk and gossip, and some of them came up to Andrew to wish him god-speed. 'Take care now, Andrew,' said one. 'We winna forget ye in a hurry, and there'll always be a welcome for ye here.'

'Dod,' said another, 'I remember the day ye put that schoolmaster in his place. Ye took the starch out o' that joker.'

'The singing in church winna be the same wi'oot ye,' said a third. 'And ye'll hev to come back for the show, and let the folks see that ye can still wrestle.'

But while they were talking Mr Charlton came over to him and said with a grave face, 'Hetherington wants a few words wi' ye, Andy.'

'What about?'

'Dinna ask me. Ye'd better not keep him waiting. Ye ken how impatient he is.'

Andrew's first thought was that the laird had found out at last that he and his uncle had stolen the hay and that he had been trespassing twice in the grounds, once to store the hay in the cave and once to get it out. As he stood waiting for the laird to speak he was more afraid than he had been before the wrestling match with Billy Craggs or when he had been fighting his way through the snow to bring back his uncle. What would happen if he was to get a summons now, just when he had written to tell his father when he would be home? Was his stay in Lilburn going 'to end not with congratulations, but with disgrace?'

'I've been hearing about you,' said Lord George. 'You are the right boy, aren't you? You look a bit on the young side to have been up to all the things I've been told about you.'

'I'm Mr Charlton's nephew, sir.'

'So you were the young feller that went up into the park and rescued him?'

'Yes, sir.'

'You did a brave thing there, very brave. How old are you?'

'Thirteen and a bit, sir.'

'Time to go to work, eh?'

'Yes, sir. Soon, sir.'

'Now I hear you're going back to your father. He's a pitman, isn't he?'

'Yes, sir.'

'Then just you take my advice, don't go. You stay here. You're just the kind of young feller I could use. I'll give you a job. And you won't find many masters better than I am. So don't forget. Off you go now. Time for dinner.'

He turned away but before Andrew could go someone else, a young man whom he had never seen before, spoke to him.

'Don't forget what my father said to you,' he said, and Andrew realized that it was Lord George's son, the young man his uncle had spoken of once. 'Mr Dennison told me a great deal about you. And I know something that my father doesn't know. You did not only save your uncle – you saved the herd as well. My father's going to leave the management of these things to me in the future and if ever there's a vacancy here I'd like you to think about it. My father doesn't bother much about the cattle, but I've made up my mind that when I'm in charge here I'll never let them get as close to perishing as they did this year. We may need you, Andrew, so don't forget us.'

The night before Andrew set out for home, caller after caller came to the cottage to wish him luck. Neighbours who had hardly seemed to notice him brought presents for his father and mother, eggs and butter and jam, and Dickie made a separate journey with a ram's horn he had carved specially for him.

There was one friend, however, who did not call – Mr Dennison. He had finished his work a long time ago and gone home. Andrew wished he could have seen him again, but his old friend did not appear.

The Miracle

Nearly a year had passed. Andrew was sitting with his father and Mr Barnes in the kitchen. Mr Robson never worked a night shift now. He had been given a light job, but even then he was easily fatigued. The injury to the legs, the many operations and the long months in hospital had taken it out of him. He never wanted to go out in the evenings, as once he did, to have a drink at the Club, or watch a game of quoits, but was content to sit in front of the fire, reading and musing, and talking to anybody who dropped in to have a word with him. Mr Barnes was the most constant visitor. Mr Robson said he was the best friend any family had ever had, and if ever there was a good angel walking on this earth it was Jack Barnes.

It was raining and the streets were deserted. The faint light of the street lamp fell on the churned-up mud between the rows and made it glisten. Once Andrew would not have minded the rain, but would have gone out in spite of it to sit with the other boys in somebody's shed or wash-house to tell stories or play with candle-ends, but not now. He had been back at Sleetburn for nearly a year, but he still had not settled. At first he had been very unhappy. Everybody made fun of the shepherd's boots that his aunt had had made for him at Lilburn. His mother had bought him a new pair, but the boys still called him by the nickname they had given him, and he smarted under their mockery. Even his own brother thought it a good joke to call him 'Bendy Leather' from time to time. Then his Aunt Florrie had unthinkingly packed his needles and wool in his bass, and he was teased mercilessly about his knitting, and about the queer Northumbrian words he had fallen into the habit of using. He had hoped that nothing in Sleetburn would have changed, but somehow it was not the place that he had left behind him.

'You'll not be long at school now, Andrew,' said Mr Barnes. 'You'll be looking for a job in a few weeks, I warrant.'

'Aye, he'll have finished his schooling come July,' said Mr Robson. 'He could have finished afore this but I want him to get a decent education, nae matter what job he gets.'

'What are you going to do with him, then?'

'I'd better get his name down for the pit. There's not much else a lad can turn to in this place.'

'How do you fancy that, Andrew?' asked Mr Barnes.

Andrew was silent.

'He can start as his brother started or mebbe get a job helping the hoss-keeper until he's ready to start as a putter. He can even be a trapper. They're always in need of trappers.'

'There's one thing I bet he'd like afore he starts,' said Mr Barnes.

'What's that, Jack?'

'A trip to Lilburn again.'

At the very mention of the word Andrew felt his heart give a jump and the blood come into his cheeks. 'I've just been thinking, Jim, that somebody should drop in on your wife's brother and tell him and his wife how grateful we were for what they did for Andrew.'

'I doubt I'm ower femmer to gan all that distance Jack.'

'I know that. And Mary Jane has plenty to do looking after the family. No, I was thinking of taking the lad up to Lilburn myself. Dinna worry about the money. I can get a few days off just about Whit and I'll pay the lad's expenses. What do

you say, Andrew? Would you like to go back and see your
Aunt Florrie again?'

Mr Barnes did not need to hear him answer. The reply was
written all over his face.

Nothing at Lilburn had changed. Everything in the familiar kitchen seemed just as it had been when Andrew had left
it – the flitches of bacon hanging, covered with pillowcases,
from the hooks in the ceiling, his uncle's razor strop on one of
the door-knobs of the dresser, the picture of Robbie Burns's
Cottage on the mantelpiece, the pots of geraniums pressing
their red flowers against the window-panes. Cappy ran out
into the yard and came back with a stick in its mouth as if not
an hour had passed since their last game together.

'Sit down the pair of ye,' said Mr Charlton. 'By gox, ye
cuddent ha' come at a better time. Something's happened
here, Andy, that's nivver happened afore. But sit ye down,
Mr Barnes. We'll be put out if ye dinna stop for two or three
days now that ye've come all this way.'

'Aye, sit down, the pair of ye,' said his wife. 'I'll put the
kettle on and give ye something to warm ye up after your
journey.'

'What's the news, Uncle?' asked Andrew.

'Oh man, the best news ye can think on. But how's
everybody at Sleetburn, Jack – I'll call ye Jack if ye dinna
mind.'

'Middling fair,' said Mr Barnes. 'Jim doesn't get what you
would call a big wage, but he gets a bit of compensation and
his eldest lad is making a good wage in the pit. They're
comfortable.'

'Well, that's good news.'

'But what about the other news, Uncle?' asked Andrew.

'Which news?'

'The good news you had to tell me.'

'Oh that. Dod, aye! What do you think – we've got two new calves!'

'But you said it was impossible.'

'It's a miracle, Andy, just a miracle. First of all one of the old heifers dropped a bull calf. By all the laws she should have stopped calving a couple of years back, but she must have come into season again. Then bless my soul, one of the young heifers went a dropped a heifer calf! Naebody's ever known a heifer have a calf at this age afore. I nivver believed in miracles afore this, Jack, but, believe me, things have happened here that have never happened in the history of the herd.'

'And what are the calves like, Uncle?'

'Beauties! The loveliest little calves ye've ever seen. I was frightened they'd turn out to be miserable specimens, because we had a terrible winter, Jack. Dod, they were all skin and bone when they came out of the snow. And the new king bull was just a young 'un that had nivver sired a calf afore. But God's good. Now we're up to fifteen, Andy – halfway back to where we were afore that awful winter. And wi' a bit of luck we'll be mair than fifteen afore the bad weather comes back again.'

'I would like to have a look at your herd, Adam,' said Mr Barnes.

'Wi' pleasure, Jack. And ye cuddent have come at a better time. The young heifer's due to present her calf to the herd tomorrow by my reckoning, and that's something that I think ye'll nivver forget if you're lucky enough to see it.'

They took the familiar track up to the park and then made their way up to the fell. The mountain turf was soft and springy, with here and there the broken shells of curlew and grouse's eggs, left lying where the chicks had wriggled out of them. As they trod on the clumps of wild thyme a fragrant smell rose in the air. Among the rough grass the harebells shook and nodded, and here and there a wild pansy pushed its yellow and purple face up through the wiry bents. From the high ground they could see Makendon Fell where the shepherd lived, with his hayfield spread out like a little green cloth on the lower slopes. Then beyond that rose the flat top of Cheviot with great white clouds sweeping over it.

They found the herd and settled down to wait for the heifer to bring her calf. It was a long wait, but in the end they saw the young heifer lead her calf out of the thicket and leave it for inspection by the king bull. Slowly and deliberately the ritual was enacted once more. The abandoned calf stood alone while the bull came ponderously over to it, paused, looked, sniffed and nudged it. A casual spectator would have seen nothing in this seemingly off-hand action, but Andrew knew that this was the moment of life or death for the calf. If the bull judged it was fit to live, it would be allowed to live. If to die, it would be mercilessly done to death by all the herd, even its own mother. He held his breath while the bull finally turned away in mute approval, and gave the signal for the rest of the herd to follow its example. Judgement had been given once more, and the verdict was life.

Mr Barnes and Andrew stayed for two more days in Lilburn. The time for cutting the peats had come round again, and they both went to the hag during the day and gave Mr Charlton a hand. It was wonderful for Andrew to be up on the fell again listening to the plovers and the curlews and the grouse calling and feeding in the wonderful sweet moorland air. Then after dark they all sat round the fire, listening to the news, how Billy Craggs had left school and gone off to work on a farm on the other side of the border, and a new schoolmaster had come to take the place of the odious Mr Ridley, and Dickie had become the champion wrestler of all Northumberland. Then, on their last evening, there was a knock on the door, and when it was opened they saw Mr

Dennison, who was on his way to Scotland to paint a picture of some wealthy client's home and had broken his journey to call on Lord Hetherington and Mr Charlton.

They all sat up very late that night, later than they had ever done since last New Year's Eve, talking about the herd and the bitter winter that had almost wiped them out.

'We'll never have to live through anything like that again, thank God,' said Mr Charlton. 'Ye've seen Hetherington, Mr Dennison?'

'Yes, I've seen him.'

'And what do you think of him?'

'I thought he had aged.'

'He's failed badly this year, but it's an ill wind that blows nobody any good. He leaves the management now to his son, and the young laird is as different from the old as chalk from cheese.'

'I know that,' said Mr Dennison. 'He thinks the world of you, Warden.'

'It's what he thinks about the herd that matters to me. And at last I have a master that sees eye to eye with me. Nae mair hunting and slaughtering. He's made up his mind to put the herd on its feet again, and by God, between us we'll do it.'

'But what about you, Andrew?' asked Mr Dennison turning to him. 'The young lord hasn't forgotten you, either. He told me what you did last winter for the cattle and for your uncle. But I suppose your mind is on other things now. Are you still at school?'

'Yes, sir, till the summer.'

'And what then?'

'His father is talking about putting him in the pit,' said Mr Barnes. 'There's not much else for a lad in Sleetburn.'

'And how do you feel, Andrew? Do you want to be a pitman?'

Andrew waited for a moment before replying. He did not

want to seem disloyal to his father, but at that moment he felt himself like the frail calf they had watched a few days ago. One word, one action, might decide his life for ever.

At last he replied.

'No, sir, I don't want to go into the pit.'

'What do you want to do, then?'

Again Andrew hesitated, but he was not undecided in his mind.

'I want to come back and work with my uncle,' he said.

'And if I have any influence,' said Mr Dennison with more emphasis than any of them had ever heard him use, 'by jingo, you will!'

A few days later Mr Robson received a letter from the young laird, offering to take on Andrew as an assistant to the Park Warden. He was offering him the job partly because he meant to see to it that the herd would grow in numbers from year to year, and partly because much extra work would be called for at a time when Mr Charlton would be the less capable of dealing with it. But these were not his only reasons.

I have a high opinion of your son, [he went on] and nobody will easily forget the fine work that he did here last winter. If it had not been for him neither the herd nor the Warden might have been with us. But I am making this offer not as a reward, but because my father and I think that Andrew will be a first-class workman. Mr Charlton, as you know, has no children of his own. It is our hope that when the time comes for him to retire he will find a successor in his nephew.

'Well, Andrew, that's a very nice letter, and I'm very proud of you, my boy,' said Mr Robson. 'What are we going to say to it?'

'I would like to go, Da.'

'You're not just frightened of the pit, are you?'

'I'm not frightened of anything.'

'I couldn't blame you if you were, lad. It hasn't done me much good. If I'd never seen it I might not be in such a poor case as I am at the present. Mr Hetherington hasn't said anything about wages. I dinna suppose you'll make as much as ye would if ye went into the pit. We get plenty fellers that give up work like this for the pits. There canna be much in it.'

'I don't care about the wage. I would rather be outside with the cattle than have to go down the pit every day.'

'What's your opinion, Jack?' said Mr Robson, turning to Mr Barnes.

'I'm not his father, Jim, and I'm not a pitman, but if you ask me, I wouldn't go down that pit for a pension. There's work for Andrew in Lilburn and that is what he fancies. Let him go. If he doesn't he could be missing the chance of a lifetime.'

'This is something I didn't bargain for, Andrew,' said Mr Robson. 'I'll have to talk it over with your mother. She winna fancy the idea of your going away again – and mebbe for good this time.'

'Even the good Lord himself had to leave his home and his family when the call came. If the call has come to Andrew let him go and answer it. And the best of good luck to you, bonny lad. I'll be sorry to see you go, but if I stood in your light I'd think a thousand shames of myself.'

The next day the decision was taken. When they were sitting together around the fire, Mrs Robson said suddenly, 'What did you do with the boots your Auntie Florrie had made for you, Andrew?'

'I've still got them, Ma. They're in the cupboard upstairs.'

'Fetch them down then, will you?'

Andrew ran upstairs and handed them over to his mother.

'They're still good boots,' she said. 'Fetch me the boot box will you?'

She spread a sheet of newspaper on the hearth and began to clean the boots, cleaning the dirt off with a knife, covering them with polish and brightening them carefully, even the hollow between the heel and the sole.

'You've kept them in good shape, I must say,' she said. 'Try them on. Do they still fit you?'

'Yes, Ma.'

'Take them then, hinny. I've had a talk with your Da, and we want you to do what we know you've set your heart on. Look after them boots, hinny, because very soon you'll be needing them again.'